The New Anne Moby

ELLEN MORGAN

The New Anne Moby

HEINEMANN : LONDON

William Heinemann Ltd
10 Upper Grosvenor Street, London W1X 9PA
LONDON   MELBOURNE   TORONTO
JOHANNESBURG   AUCKLAND
First published 1985
© Kathleen M. Bumstead 1985
434 95165 X

Printed in Great Britain by
Mackays of Chatham

Chapter 1

Anne was standing in the corridor. Again. She watched the sun streaming through the glass of the classroom door, and the dust motes danced in the light. No wonder, the floor was dull and dusty. Dirty. And the walls were a nasty yellowish-white, with dirty white showing through where the paint had been picked off. And the network of pipes under the ceiling was ugly and dull. She was bored. It had happened so often, her being sent out to stand there; she had exhausted all the possible things to do to pass the time. She had learned not to approach the classroom door and pull faces – that had brought awful retribution. She had spent times drawing patterns in the dust and playing a miniature hop-scotch; but her shoes squeaked and she was caught at that and punished again. She had tried drawing pictures and letters on the dust and damp of the wall, but that was called 'vandalism' and 'graffity', whatever that was, and she was punished again. So really there was nothing for it but to wait, easing her back against the wall, finding the most comfortable way of standing.

The drone of voices came through the closed doors. Dare she edge along and just peep in from the side? It would be something to do. But she'd have to be very, very careful, the teachers were on the look-out for her trying it and distracting the others. As quick to pounce as a cat they were! But it would be something to manage it despite them.

She began to edge towards the next door. Perhaps that teacher didn't know she'd been sent out again, and wouldn't be looking for her.

She slid along the wall, but all she could see was the classroom wall, high up over everyone's heads. That wasn't any use. It didn't count. She must see right inside to win.

It meant exposing the very least bit of herself possible. She scraped her untidy hair back even tighter behind her ear, and tilted her head at an angle so that her eye would be level with the glass with a tiny bit of her head showing. Slowly. Quick movement was seen easier. Very slowly. She'd almost won . . .

A door closed noisily and heavy footsteps approached the end of the corridor. Anne drew back like a snake's head retracting; but guilt was written all over her posture and the uneasy expression on her face.

It was Mrs Timmins, the Headmistress. Short, cropped hair; heavy body, shapeless cardigan, heavy shoes . . .

'What are you doing out here, Anne Moby?'

It was no use trying to tell a fib, she'd tried that before, and they knew – if it was her – it wasn't true, and you copped it worse.

'Please, Miss Smith sent me out, Mrs Timmins.'

'Again! You must be the worst behaved child in the school. I don't know what'll become of you! Come with me and we'll see what you've been up to this time.'

This was awful. It was worse than the sting of the cane. That was soon over, and only another hurt among a lot of hurts that happened. But to be taken back and shown up before all the class, and told off and sneered at while the rest of the class laughed at her to toady up to the teachers –

that was awful. It hurt inside like a great heavy weight. It almost made her cry, which would be the worst shame and horror. And it made her angry, red, blind, blazing angry, till she didn't remember what it was wise to do or say, and did the sort of things that had given her a bad name. Saying things that shouldn't be said to teachers, with words you shouldn't know; pulling to get free ... unallowable things.

It was just like that. Back they went into the sunshine of the classroom. There was the usual inquisition. Anne tried not to listen. Just wait, that was best. Not listen, and not care.

'I was speaking to you, Anne Moby!'

Anne didn't know what had been said, and so could not answer. She just looked steadily at the flushed face towering above her, instead.

'You insolent creature!' spluttered Mrs Timmins. 'Come with me!'

She grasped Anne by the scrawny arm and dragged her out of the room. The door closed on the subdued titter of the class. The undignified march up the corridor ended in the Headmistress's room. It smelt revoltingly of cigarette ends from the tray of stubs on the table. The hand holding Anne so firmly was yellow-stained with nicotine and wrinkled.

'Put out your hand!'

Anne had no alternative.

The heavy ruler came down relentlessly, leaving a red weal.

'Ouch!' Anne cried.

Just as the school secretary opened the door to announce the arrival of one of the school inspectors.

Anne was hurriedly dismissed. It was no use making for the cloakroom; it was nearly dinner time, and they would all be coming out, and they would see her marked hand, and even that she'd nearly cried. She hadn't a coat. She ran outside, out of the school gates and down the road.

Home. Home for the last few weeks, anyway. Ma would be at work, and 'Dad' asleep. She crept in, nursing her hurt hand under the opposite armpit to warm it, but it still hurt.

There was no fire. 'Dad' was snoring. There was a crust by the sink. She ate it hungrily. Then she'd better leave before they found she'd been home and pinched the crust. She rummaged out an old coat, too untidy for school; and still nursing her hand, went out softly, down the road and into the bit of woodland where the lads raced bikes of a night.

She never knew of the small revolution she had brought about. Before Mrs Timmins took 'early retirement' as the best option left to her, Anne's mother had received an official looking letter.

'Read that, while I get a cup of tea,' her mother ordered when she came in from work, kicking her shoes off to rest her feet.

Anne opened the letter carefully.

'Dear Mrs Moby,' she read.
'In view of the problems occ-as-ioned by your daughter's behaviour at Greenside School, it has been thought advisable to transfer her to Morton Hill School, Hill Lane.

She should start there on Monday, 14 March.
Yours faithfully,
M E Timmins
Headmistress'

Anne finished triumphantly. Some of the words had been long and unfamiliar, but she thought she had got it right. All those long words about her! She must be important. And such an elegant letter!

'Dad' came into the room, scratching himself and yawning. The worst of shift work was you never felt fresh when you woke up, always frowsy and as if you hadn't had your sleep out.

'What's that?' he asked suspiciously, pointing to the letter.

'It's from the school. About our Anne.'

'She's none of mine!' he disclaimed hurriedly. 'Your problem that is.'

Anne knew that her real father had died long ago, before she could remember. She didn't like this man she was told to call 'Dad', and avoided him as much as she could. Now she helped herself to a mug of tea and sidled out on to the balcony. Every flat in the block had a concrete balcony, for drying the washing. A flapping shirt and a pair of socks almost got in her tea. She brushed them aside distastefully, keeping a wary ear on the rising voices inside the room. This didn't sound like a really bad 'do', but you never knew. Sometimes when they had finished with each other, they turned on her. Ma wasn't so bad, though she hit harder than Mrs Timmins – and just with her hand, too. But when 'Dad' took off his leather belt and drew it through his hand, it was time to run. Fast.

She put her empty mug on the table and slid like a shadow round the edges of the room and out to the common. There she passed the time whistling tunelessly and shuffling her feet through the litter of paper and cartons and last year's leaves until the others came out to play. By the time she went in, 'Dad' would have left for work.

Meanwhile, Jimmy Reed might let her ride his bike, like he'd promised last night . . .

Chapter 2

Next Monday morning Anne set out for Morton Hill School. She knew where it was because when she and Ma first moved to Mill Road she'd ranged all the streets round to find what they offered. She knew all the fish-and-chippies and the cinemas, the shops selling TVs where you could stand outside and see the pictures, and the parks and playgrounds. The schools had just happened along incidentally. And with nine schools already behind her, she was something of a connoisseur, and looked new ones over just in case.

Morton Hill was more than two miles away. No one had given her a bus pass and she knew she'd never get past the driver without one, so she walked. Ma hadn't thought of that, and hadn't got her up early enough. So she'd be late. Oh well. So she'd be late.

It was a fine morning, with the sun trying to shine through low mist. She waved at the greengrocer as she passed, and felt a bit more cheerful.

Anne looked at the buses passing, and the clothes of the women. There were a couple of good-looking older boys in school uniform, carrying attaché cases. She noticed the cruel way the tree at the corner had been cut back because of the traffic. She tried not to walk on the lines between the paving stones. Then she tried to balance on the kerb. She sang under her breath and walked in time with the tune. It was a really nice walk.

And then she was at the school.

She stopped and looked at it. It was big – as usual – and old – as usual. With railings round a grotty playground. As usual. But something was a bit different. It was the flowers. The beds under the windows had been dug properly and there were daffies in bud. It was ages and ages since she'd seen daffies really growing, not just picked and lying in the shops in tight bundles in boxes. She walked past them slowly, wishing she dared touch. Just once. They looked so cool and clean and – special. But she'd better begin right. Feeling very virtuous, she passed on without even the smallest attempt at a touch, though there seemed no one to see.

There were several doors and she wandered from one to the other, wondering which she should use. One was standing open, so she chose that, went inside and found herself in a corridor. But this was different from the last school. It was as old as anything, of course – just brick walls with high windows, like they all were. But these bricks were painted blue at the bottom and white higher up – gleaming pale blue and white. And there was a board with paintings on, looking like proper pictures with frames round them, even if the frames were only made from coloured paper. Pictures of flowers and animals – a cat – that one was really good. She wandered along, examining them.

A young lady suddenly came round the corner and saw Anne. 'What do you want?' she asked.

Anne looked guilty. Probably she'd come in the wrong way, or shouldn't be looking at the pictures, or something.

'I'm Anne Moby,' she said, much less aggressively than she usually spoke to 'Them'. 'I'm to come to this school.'

'Oh yes,' said the school secretary. 'There was a letter

8

about you this morning. Just wait a minute while I ring the bell.'

She went to the end of the corridor and rang the bell vigorously. Doors opened, and Anne stood flat to the wall while children streamed past her, making for the playground. Some were digging in their pockets for sweets and biscuits, and Anne remembered she'd had no break-fast as hunger cramped her skinny middle.

'Now,' said the secretary, when the crowd had passed. 'Come along to Miss Garfield.'

Well, it had to be got over with, hadn't it? They never knocked you about the first time they saw you. Perhaps they wouldn't say anything very awful either, though they must know what had happened at the other school if there'd been a letter. She straightened her frock as best she could, and wished she was wearing socks instead of just shoes.

The secretary knocked at the door and a voice called for them to go in.

The first thing Anne saw was the most lovely bowl of flowers, right in front of her. There were daffies full out – and red flowers – tulips? – and feathery yellow stuff she didn't know, and it all smelled like heaven. She forgot where she was and just stood and looked, and without even having to sniff she was surrounded by fragrance.

'This is Anne Moby,' the secretary explained. 'Mr Martin came about her yesterday afternoon. She's to start here.'

'Oh yes,' said the large lady behind the desk. But this was a soft, warm, largeness, and the woolly cardigan was soft and pink, and the grey hair looked soft too. She had her arm round a boy as skinny as Anne, who was sitting beside her. He had his arm in a sling.

'Run along now, Jimmy,' said Miss Garfield. 'I'll hear

9

you read another time instead. All right?'

Jimmy nodded and slid away.

'He broke his arm two days ago, so he can't go out to play yet,' Miss Garfield explained. 'So I hear him read while we have the chance, don't I, Jimmy?'

Jimmy turned at the door and nodded.

'Now – you are Anne Moby?'

'Yes, Miss.'

'You like my flowers?'

'Yes, Miss.'

'It was my birthday yesterday and they were a present, so I brought them to school so that I could see them in the daytime. Now, you are ten years old, Anne? You'd better start in Mrs Wood's class. They say your maths are poor.'

Anne thought it was best to stay silent. If they were really telling from her last school, all her work was poor, she knew.

'Can you read, Anne? Will you read this to me?'

She rummaged in her desk and brought out a book. Nice and clean it was, with a proper cover on. Anne took it gingerly.

'Just start at the beginning.'

Anne coulc read. She'd found that the only way to know what the stories were about was to read them for herself. Sometimes she had found a library to go to. And it meant she knew what was on the telly. It hadn't been hard to learn. Somehow, as far back as she could remember she had been able to read. So she read confidently from the lovely clean book.

'Good. Very good. Now, writing. Just write your name and address here for me, will you?'

This was bad. Writing was something she had never tried at and it looked awful and was spelt wrong all the time too. She never managed more than a couple of lines, and then there was trouble. Such daft things they asked you to write! 'A Composition on Last Night.' Wouldn't half be a scene if she really told them what had happened at their place last night! But she wished now she could do something better than scrawl.

'Anne Moby,' the Headmistress deciphered. 'Is that A-n-n-e?'

Anne nodded. 'I spell it like that,' she said defiantly.

She nearly always had this fight. Somehow it was important that she had an 'e' on the end, like people in her favourite stories. But the schools almost always wouldn't have it, as if three letters were quite enough for her.

'This letter says A-n-n,' said the Headmistress. 'But perhaps they made a mistake, so we'll put an "e" on the end for now anyway.'

And so it went on. No loud voices. No nagging. Where was the catch?

Anne found herself in a sunny classroom – only a partition from the one next door so that you heard noise through, and the desk was old-fashioned and chipped a bit. But it was all clean and bright and there were bulbs growing on the window sill. There was hardly space for her to sit down, the room was so crowded, but no one seemed to mind the crush.

When dinner-time came, Mrs Wood noticed her hang back when the others went to wash their hands. She hadn't a ticket. Or any money. There were whispered consultations. Then she was taken through and sat down and given a dinner.

Later there was a bus pass for next day.

The sun seemed to shine and shine.

It was too good to be true.

And they ended with a story.

Anne wandered home, her eyes on the pavement,

reliving all the splendid things – the painted corridor – the bowl of flowers – the pretty new book – the dinner! – the help when she couldn't do her sums. The story . . .

'Please can it go on?' she whispered.

But of course it didn't. Only a week later she missed the bus because Ma had stayed out all night and wasn't there to wake her. So Anne missed part of the maths lesson just when they were doing something new and hard. There wasn't time for Mrs Wood to explain it again to a late-comer with so many others needing attention, and in the end not a single sum was right.

The day got worse as it went along. Mrs Wood hadn't liked her getting so many sums wrong, somehow good-ness and sums-right went together, and she felt bad because of her failure. Others had had difficulties too and felt the same. And then Anne got really naughty. Drawing meaningless squiggles when she should have been writing her spellings. Pulling a face at the girl in the next desk – and what a face! Mrs Wood wasn't easily shocked, but that was – evil! The girl seemed a restless, malicious change-ling. And she raised the devil in the others too. It was always there, but when things were going well, it wasn't much in evidence. With Anne Moby behaving like this, other small devils in other small bodies raised their heads as they recognised a familiar spirit. Mary Macdonald was caught throwing her rubber across the room. Sam Peters kept pulling out his neighbour's shirt-tail . . . Would the morning never end?

The afternoon was no better. Someone upset a jar of water over Margaret's painting that she was so proud of. No need to look far to find it had been Anne Moby. When all that was mopped up, it was playtime, and some of them hadn't finished, with all the disturbances. They were given more time, but the enthusiasm and atmosphere were gone – some tried to read, but couldn't settle to it while others were traipsing to and fro. They got bored and the tricks started again.

Anne Moby didn't do anything else wrong that anyone could see. It was the others. And yet somehow it all stemmed from Anne. The girl was so clever at it, so skilful, the teacher never caught more than the tail-end of a glance that egged on another child to insubordination. Look hard at Anne, and she was as straight-faced as a plaster image, if a rather grubby one. It was three o'clock before Mrs Wood, turning very quickly, caught Anne at her mischief, out of her place, doing a rude disco-type dance in the aisle between the desks. But Anne was so quick that she was seated again with a dutiful expression on her face almost immediately. Mrs Wood could hardly believe what she had seen.

'Stay in after school and see me, Anne Moby,' she said.

She realised with relief that that was it. It was Anne getting away with her mischief all day long that had stirred the others up. Now she had been caught, the others became as good as they usually were. With her confidence restored, the teacher had the painting things cleared away in no time, everyone seated properly, and there was time for ten minutes of a story after all.

'Good afternoon, children . . .'

'Good afternoon, Mrs Wood . . .'

A clatter as the chairs were heaved on top of the desks to leave the floor clear for the cleaners; a fiddlement as Johnny came for the money she'd been keeping for him, and Marlene for her special book, and Sammy because his shoe-lace had broken and Tim because he couldn't find one of his wellingtons . . .

At last it was quiet and rather cold.

And no Anne Moby.

She'd gone off with the others, in spite of being told to stay.

Mrs Wood sighed.

As a matter of fact, Anne was as unhappy as Mrs Wood. No one on the bus seemed to find her antics amusing . . . and then she was scuffing her way along the pavement by herself. Even the greengrocer was busy with a customer and didn't notice her. She took the key from the string round her neck and opened the door to the flat.

The windows had been closed all day, and the smell was horrible. Last night's dishes were still there – so Ma hadn't come home yet. And no sign of 'Dad'. Anne put the kettle on for a drink of tea and rummaged for some bread – but the bit of butter left was an oily mess and she scraped out a jam jar instead. Eventually she sat drinking her tea, eating her butty, and thinking – reluctantly – about the day.

It had happened again.

Often she started to be 'good', but she always ended being 'bad'. This time she especially hadn't meant to. She really liked that school, and she'd meant to go regularly and do what they said. And now she'd got Mrs Wood angry. And perhaps Miss Garfield would hear of it.

All right, she'd won. She'd got away with it almost all day. It was a difficult, dangerous game, and those who blamed her for it didn't realise you needed skill and a lot of nerve to play it. They ought to have a go themselves! And she hadn't got sent out. She hadn't even got shouted at.

So why did she feel she'd lost after all?

She scratched her itchy elbows and wriggled uncomfortably. She wished today hadn't happened.

It was Ma's fault. If she'd been got up at the proper time

she wouldn't have been late for school and got all her sums wrong.

Where was Ma, anyway?

She poured another cup of tea and switched the telly on.

Later she went out and found some of her friends. It was a fine evening and they played 'catch' on the wasteland, until it grew dark and they were called in to their supper.

No one called Anne.

She used her key to get in the flat again. Flies were buzzing in the window. Still no one was home. It seemed a long time since school dinner, and she was hungry again. She hadn't any money for fish-and-chips, and although she searched everywhere she couldn't find any – none in the drawer – none on the mantelpiece – none by the gas meter. She went into 'their' room to see if there was anything left in a pocket, but Ma's jacket wasn't there, not the one she usually wore. Or her hat. Anne was startled. That hadn't happened before. 'Dad' never seemed to have much besides the clothes he stood up in, but Ma had her working clothes and her going-out clothes, as well as the old clothes she wore to clean up the flat. That was all that was left now – the old slacks and jumper.

Where was Ma, anyway? It was nine o'clock.

Anne switched the light on, half her mind on how hungry she was, half worrying about what might have happened to Ma. Had she been in an accident?

What should she do? For a moment she thought of going to the police but that wouldn't do. She'd get in awful trouble if she got Ma mixed up with the police. All right, her mother wasn't all that, but you didn't have to tell everyone, and Ma was hers and all she'd got, and she could be real nice sometimes.

She found a small tin of beans that had fallen at the back of the cupboard so she had that for her supper. She sat up gazing at TV, expecting every minute to hear Ma's key in the lock. Then it was eleven o'clock. She washed her face and went to bed, hoping she'd wake in time in the morning.

She kept waking through the night, and listening. After seven o'clock she didn't dare go to sleep again in case she was late. She got up and made tea – the milk was sour so she had it without and it left brown marks on the mug – and was early for the bus for once.

She looked just as she always did – perhaps a little paler even than usual. But inside she felt like a traveller in a strange land, cut off from all known support, and in dire peril.

Chapter 3

Anne was so quiet at school that day that fleetingly, as her other charges gave her the chance to notice between their constant demands, Mrs Wood was concerned. She seemed to be far away, thinking of something else. At least she was not the slightest trouble! But the pale face with a frown between the dark eye-brows, drawing them together until they almost met, attracted her attention increasingly as the day wore on. She denied that she was ill, and seemed startled to be asked. She was not a child to make a fuss about nothing, but those thin shoulders seemed to be bearing an intolerable load of responsibility.

When school was over, Mrs Wood took her problem to Miss Garfield.

'Trouble at home,' she diagnosed. 'Thank you for telling me. I'll try to see her tomorrow.'

Meanwhile, Anne left the bus and loitered up the street, almost frightened of what she would find when she opened the door. Of course Ma would be home!

But suppose she wasn't?

And she wasn't. Just the stuffy flat, flies in the window, dirty dishes . . . Anne flung the window open and tackled the dishes, boiling up some water for the job. Ma would expect her – at her age – to manage for a day or so, and she'd better tidy up, or there'd be trouble when they came back and found nothing done. She put the dishes away and felt

17

more cheerful. Until she went into their bedroom and found Ma's clothes still all gone except the old ones.

What had happened? What should she DO?

It was worse that night. There really was nothing at all left to eat; and the gas gave out so she couldn't even boil the kettle again. She didn't feel like going out to play. She watched telly doggedly. And at last crept into bed, wishing hard that she knew what to do, or had someone to ask.

Miss Garfield sent for Anne the next morning. Compassion smote her as she looked at the skinny legs and rather grimy knees and ankles and scuffed shoes, the steady grey eyes in the pinched white face, under such fierce eye-brows. Everything about her suggested a hard life where she had had to fight her own fights. And now? Mrs Wood had been right. There was some bigger battle that daunted even her.

'Sit down, Anne,' she said kindly.

Anne's heart plummeted. Why had she been sent for? Was there some news? Was it bad? Was this how they told you?

'What is it?' asked Miss Garfield, sensing the child's rising panic.

Anne kept quiet. Surely it wasn't news; they wouldn't keep her waiting like this else? And she wasn't going to tell tales. Besides, it might be all right when she got home tonight . . .

The silence lengthened. The secretary knocked discreetly at the door, bringing coffee and biscuits.

'Another cup of coffee please, Mary,' said Miss Garfield.

And so they sat opposite each other, Anne relishing the fabulously fragrant drink, treating the saucer with care, only taking two biscuits so it wouldn't show she was starving hungry . . . It was quiet. The spring air came in through the open window and sparrows chirped in the bushes outside.

'Well,' said Miss Garfield, putting down her cup. 'What is the trouble? And don't tell me there isn't any, because I know there is.'

How can she know, unless she knows where Ma is? wondered Anne – though she didn't really put any miracle much beyond Miss Garfield. Should she tell? Was this the person she'd been looking for to ask? She almost opened her mouth to pour out the whole story, but at the last minute she changed her mind. One more day! It might be all right tonight. Nothing bad could have happened or she'd be told. It wasn't fair to Ma to tell tales – and what would Miss Garfield think?

She kept silent.

'If you do have a problem, you will come and tell me, won't you?'

'Yes,' lied Anne.

And then the bell rang for break and she was allowed to go.

Anne thought her deception had worked; but really it had only increased Miss Garfield's alarm. Something was wrong, and the child wouldn't admit it. And she was such a waif – only as thick as a piece of paper, with a shock of dark hair at one end and over-large shoes at the other – and such delicate hands, holding her saucer so carefully.

So at dinner-time Miss Garfield got in her car and drove to the address on Anne's school card. She stopped at the block of flats, standing in its dingy patch of shorn grass; and found the number she wanted; but there was no reply to her ring or knock. That might not mean anything; both parents might well be out at work. She glanced along the corridor with distaste. Ugly concrete! Dirty, littered floor!

19

Chipped walls. Nasty smell. What the bairns in her care had to cope with before they came near school! Only the warmth of family affection could bring life to these sterile surroundings, where nothing grew, nothing real, natural and lovely seemed ever to have been.

One of the neighbouring doors opened, but when she asked the woman if she knew where she could find Mrs Moby, the answer was negative and the door firmly closed again. She tried two more doors, but there was no answer. She looked for a caretaker but couldn't find one. The mission was a failure.

It was time for afternoon school, and she must go back. She was a little ashamed of the relief she felt at finding her car unmolested; and to find it so nice and comfortable to be in its warm, clean seat again. Her own room seemed luxurious as she took off her coat. She felt such thoughts were unworthy. Most of her pupils came from the area she had just visited. Most of them managed very well. She marvelled again at the resilience of the young.

Then she turned to the work on her desk. There seemed nothing else she could do, unless she could find real proof that something was wrong.

At seven o'clock that evening, Anne heard a knock at the door and she hurried to open it. News of Ma at last perhaps?

She saw Miss Garfield against the dingy background of the corridor.

For a moment neither of them spoke. They seemed like different people, meeting out of school like this, as if they had never seen each other clearly before.

Miss Garfield pulled herself together.

'Is your mother at home, Anne?'

'No, Miss Garfield.'

Anne stood firmly in the doorway.

'Could I come in and wait for her?'

'I don't know when she'll be back.'

How true that was, Anne thought bitterly. She shivered, for the evening had turned cold. She had had double helpings of everything at dinner, but that seemed a long time ago, and she was beginning to worry about how she could get enough to eat. Today was Thursday – there was only Friday, and then two days with no school and so no dinner. She had been thinking of that when Miss Garfield knocked. Only one more day, and then she'd have to find where beggars went to; or steal; and mostly people got caught when they stole and sent off into Care. She'd have to think of something, quick. And she mustn't let Miss Garfield see the state the flat was in.

But Miss Garfield was somehow coming through the door and it was somehow not possible to prevent it.

'Now, Anne,' she said firmly, sitting down on the most serviceable looking chair. 'Let's have no more nonsense. Where is your mother?'

'I expect she's at work . . .' Anne said hesitatingly.

'Shall I light the fire?'

'There's no gas.'

'Is it out of order, or does it want something in the meter?'

'Got no money.'

'Well, I have. Show me where it is.'

And so, since Miss Garfield luckily had a box of matches, they got the fire lit.

'That's better. Now, when do you think your mother will be home?'

'Don't know.'

'What time is she usually back?' Miss Garfield asked.

'About five.'

'But it's seven o'clock now!'

Everything Anne said, and everything Miss Garfield saw, strengthened the suspicion that Anne was alone, and didn't know where her mother was. Just then there was some commotion outside, and a loud knocking at the door. Anne hurried to open it, and two men walked in.

'You Mrs Moby?' they asked, looking at Miss Garfield with some surprise.

'No. Can I help you?'

'We've come to take the telly away.'

'Why? Does it need mending?'

The man grinned.

'Naw. They never paid nothin' on it for weeks, that's what.'

The second man was busy disconnecting wires, and they rapidly picked up the set and left. Before Anne could close the door, another stranger, a younger man, looked in.

'Are you Mrs Moby?' he, too, asked hesitatingly, looking at the elegant clothes and handbag.

'No. I'm Anne's Headmistress.'

'I'm John Lambert. Social worker. Greenside School asked me to call.'

Anne hurriedly shut the door. Not that she'd ever live this down. Someone calling from school, them taking the telly away and everyone hearing they were behind with the payments; and now the Social lot. Were all these disasters somehow her fault? What should she have done?

Miss Garfield and John Lambert talked easily. This was the sort of problem they were both used to – poverty – shifting personal relationships – and children stranded in the rough seas of adult affairs. Anne had almost become a 'case', a 'statistic'. The smooth voices talked on, quickly and quietly, and Anne felt a panic sense of her life being arranged for her, and out of her hands . . . What would happen to her? She burst out with what seemed to her the one important thing.

'WHERE'S MY MA?'

Miss Garfield was brought suddenly back to reality.

'We don't know, Anne. But we'll try to find her. When did you last see her?'

'Monday.'

'We'll check the hospitals,' John Lambert said. 'But we'd have heard if there'd been an accident. Where did your mother work?'

'She was a cleaner at the Town Hall.'

'It's too late to ask there tonight; everyone will have gone home. Just you and your mother, was there?'

'There was "Dad". They told me to call him Dad, but he wasn't really. He worked nights.'

'When did you last see him?'

'Sunday.'

It was growing dark, and Anne moved to put the light on. As she did so, she heard a key in the door.

'Ma!' she called joyfully. The awful responsibility of managing on her own was ended!

But the door opened to show the skinny, harassed figure of the caretaker of the flats.

'Caught you at last!' he said, peering at Miss Garfield. And then, puzzled, he said, 'You're not Mrs Moby!' And, looking at the other visitor, 'And you're not her bloke!'

There were more explanations. Anne retreated to the window again.

'Well, they've paid no rent for three weeks; they'll have to go,' she heard the caretaker say in a mock-valiant voice.

Anne felt it had got beyond her, there were too many problems, too much wrong. Should she cut and run for it?

But where to? And how would Ma ever find her when – if – she came back, if she'd cleared off? These people were probably the only ones who could get them all together again.

'The problem,' Miss Garfield was saying firmly, 'is to get Anne properly cared for and to find her mother.'

'Looks as if she's cleared off. Finding her might take some time.'

'She wouldn't go and leave Anne!'

'Wouldn't she just? It happens all the time.'

Anne didn't know which hurt most, being hungry, or thinking that Ma had gone off and left her to manage as best she could.

'Have you any relatives?'

She shook her head.

'Where did you live before you came here?'

'Liversedge. And Bradford before that. And the other side of Leeds. And Huddersfield. I can't remember before that.'

Anne thought she would never forget the spluttering gas fire, the white glare of the electric light, the familiar face and form of Miss Garfield, the other two strangers standing and talking, while all her life was smashed up. No more Ma. No 'Dad' even. No more familiar room and cups of tea and the sight and smell and feel of things and people that belonged with her.

'Anne had better come home with me,' said Miss Garfield. It wasn't what she wanted, but she felt she must make the offer as the least she could do.

'Better not,' advised John Lambert. 'It might be for a long time. And if you do it for one, you'll be expected to do it again. Besides, she'll settle better with others her own age. We've a hostel for emergencies like this. She can stay there while we make some enquiries.'

'Hostel!' Dreaded word. All part of being 'taken into Care'; the disaster akin to prison or a fatal disease, in the talk she'd heard. But the prospect of living with Miss Garfield was in some ways even more alarming.

'Well, if you're not happy, you must tell me, Anne, and I'll arrange something else.' Miss Garfield tried to keep any shade of relief out of her feelings as well as out of her voice. She was half-glad to be relieved of the responsibility, and half-concerned that perhaps she should do more.

'I can still come to your school?'

'Yes, we'll arrange that,' John Lambert agreed. 'Get your things now, and we'll be on our way – we should get there in time for supper.'

Anne revived at that magic word, and went into her room to get her few clothes and her bag of treasures. There was no suitcase – Ma must have taken it – so they wrapped her things in newspaper while she carried the plastic bag that held her empty scent bottle, a picture of Michael Jackson, the red ribbon from a chocolate box and a one franc piece she had once found.

The room seemed bare without the telly. The caretaker turned off the gas fire. Anne took a last look round – the empty cupboard door standing open – the tear in the carpet where Ma always caught her heel . . . And then they left. The light was switched off and the door locked. It was very final.

Then they were in the street, going their separate ways. The caretaker walked shakily off round the corner. Miss Garfield squeezed Anne's hand, got into her car and drove off.

And Anne, with her newspaper parcel and her plastic bag, got into the van beside John Lambert, and set out for the next stage of a life which already in ten years had provided so many crises and changes.

The street lights were bright and gay. The tyres swished on the wet road.

At least they'd said she'd have some supper.

And Ma might come back . . .

Chapter 4

The next few weeks were so horrid that afterwards Anne refused to think about them, and so in a way forgot them. No one was downright unkind to her, and she had enough to eat. But she hated never being alone, even if she did have a nightie and bed-clothes now. She hated the 'leastness' of everything – the formica-topped tables, metal-backed chairs, plain linoleum on the floor, blinds instead of curtains. There was just enough of everything and nothing special at all. She tried to explain this to Miss Garfield when she was taken into her room and given a cup of coffee again. Miss Garfield noticed how her fingers stroked the pretty china and her eyes strayed to the inevitable bowl of flowers on the desk.

'Come and see me before you go home tonight, Anne,' she said, understanding more from watching than from listening to the halting words.

And at home-time, Anne was given three narcissi, dazzling white like in a TV advert or the Angel Gabriel's robe, and scented like heaven. She kept them for days in a jam-jar by her bed, changing the water night and morning, until the white freshness became paper thin and the scent changed. Then she walked to the park and laid them under some bushes. She couldn't bear to think of them thrown in a dustbin with empty tins of cat food and other rubbish.

'Daft!' she admonished herself, walking back to the hostel in the twilight.

At first she hoped every morning and every night when she got back from school that there would be word of Ma. It wasn't that Ma had ever been very kind to her, or made much of a fuss, and if she'd been crossed she'd often say, 'I'll put you in Care, that's what I'll do!' And now she had left her to be taken into Care. But she was the only human being who had always been there, who belonged.

John Lambert, the social worker, came to see her again. She couldn't stay in the hostel indefinitely, her place was needed; and he realised that she was particularly unsuited to life in an institution. Some didn't mind it so much, but Anne did, increasingly and passionately.

'Did your mother never mention any relatives at all?' he asked.

She shook her head.

'What about your Dad?'

'He got killed ever so long ago.'

'You've no aunties and uncles? No granny?'

She shook her head again, but the experienced Mr Lambert detected the merest shadow of hesitation.

'What is it?'

'Well – I asked if I hadn't a granny once, when they'd been talking about it at school. And Ma said, 'Not really.' So I asked her what did she mean and she said she'd left home a long time ago and Nana would be gone long since because she'd be over seventy now.'

Anne's voice expressed her wonder at this enormous age.

'She didn't say where Nana lived?'

'In the country somewhere. She said it was funny because the most important name in the place was something like hers.'

'What was your Dad's name?'

'Ma called him Jack.'

'And you've always been Anne Moby?'

Anne nodded.

John Lambert took his problem to Miss Garfield.

'You see Moby is the only name we have to go on. We don't know if the mother married Anne's father or not – so we can only look for relatives called Moby. The family moved so much, and no one seems to know where they came from. The only clue we have is that Anne says it was in the country. And this about a famous name . . .'

'The most important name there . . . it's like a fairy story, isn't it? A riddle we must solve if Anne is to live happily ever after . . .'

'Some riddle! It looks as if the family lived in Yorkshire, but that's a big place to start looking. I've tried all the usual things, but there aren't many Mobys, and none of those I've found knows anything about Anne's family.'

'We can only try,' said Miss Garfield, thoughtfully.

The problem lingered at the back of her mind for the rest of the day; and in the evening she got down her collection of maps. It was no use looking for a village on a big map; it would have to be the large-scale Ordnance Survey ones. But what a lot of villages there were!

She started with the Tourist Map of the North York moors. But there were hardly any names beginning with 'M'. Maltby. It couldn't be that.

She put that map away and tried Wensleydale instead. Here were more 'Ms'. Melmerby. Middleham. Marrick. Malham. Mewith Head. Muker. None of them could be made to sound like Moby.

But Anne hadn't said it was the name of a village – only that it was in the country and the most important name there . . . it could be the most important family instead.

Perhaps she was on the wrong tack and should be looking at books of heraldry, or the peerage – where rich and important families were mentioned.

She thought she would try one more map – the one of lower Wensleydale. Sheet 99.

Funny names again – Sweet Earth – Benny Bent . . . but LOTS of 'Ms' too. Masham. Monk Ing. Merryfield. Magdalene Wood. Mickley. There was enough room on the map for individual farms to be mentioned – Mossy Mire House. What a picture of winter mud on boots and squelching bogs round the stack-yard that conjured up.

Mowbray House. Mowbray Hall. That sounded more like 'important people'. And it began with M-o-. Miss Garfield muttered it to herself. Mowbray. Moby. Mobry. Moby-Mobry-Mowbray . . .

The next evening she settled down to look at a very old local history book borrowed from a friend. She turned first to a photograph, taken many years ago – 'The Vale of Mowbray from Well Village'. It showed a delightful landscape . . . she would certainly go there one weekend.

Then she turned to the text:

'Just on the north entrance of the river gorge is Mowbray Wath, Wath meaning a ford, a spot where the river might be waded . . .

Kirkeby was formerly a market town, its market being granted first to John de Mowbray in 1307, by Edward I . . . Soon after the Conquest a castle was reared at this place by Robert de Mowbray whose son, Roger de Mowbray, was a renowned warrior and fought at the celebrated Battle of the Standard, being at that period only a youth. For having joined in a rebellion against Henry II, 1173, his castles at Kirkeby and Thirsk were beseiged and afterwards dismantled by order of the monarch . . .'

Well, there it was. It was an 'important name' all right, going back to Norman times, with castles and everything. And it did sound like Moby. It just might be . . .

'The granny is probably dead,' Miss Garfield reminded herself. 'Or too old to cope with Anne. Even if it is the proper place and I find her.'

But she could hardly wait for the weekend all the same.

Miss Garfield wondered whether or not to take Anne with her. In a way it would be dreadful to raise false hopes. On the other hand the granny, if there was one, might be struck by some family resemblance – or Anne might just remember something else her mother had told her. She decided to go alone. Anne was too quick witted not to see what was in the wind if something so extraordinary as being taken out by her Headmistress for the day was suggested, to seek an old woman with a name like her own. It would be cruel to raise hopes only to dash them.

It was thirty miles to Kirkeby, but the car was going well, and the weather was glorious. She felt lucky. Surely everything would go right on such a lovely day? Driving through the market town of Ripon she became discouraged – so many people crowding the pavements, walking in the road, clustering round the market stalls, parking cars, trying to park cars . . . What hope was there of finding one relative – even if she did exist – of one deserted child? It was a fool's errand.

But as she passed into the countryside again her confidence returned. There, between the ancient hedgerows, the old field boundaries, grew the oak and ash trees that were descendants of other oaks and ashes, and the ancestors, with luck, of generations more – the past did not seem so far away, nor the world such a big place. She passed a farmhouse dyed soft yellow with the local ochre colour wash, its small-paned windows drawn open to the good air. Ahead she suddenly saw the line of the moors, only about five miles away. There was a sign post that said: Kirkeby 2¼ miles. For the first time since she had read the name in that history book she felt it was a real place, not a name in a story she was making up.

In a few minutes she was driving up the village street. She decided to look for the post office and ask there for a Mrs Moby.

It was ridiculously easy.

'Yes,' said the busy postmistress. 'In Church Street. Which way have you come? Well, turn round and go back to the crossroads, and you'll see the church. Mrs Moby lives in the little cottage almost opposite the gates.'

So many doubts and such impossible seeming difficulties – and now all at once it was all unravelling like a tangled skein of wool. John Lambert had said there weren't many Mobys in the whole county – so surely there was at least a chance that the one here, where Mowbray had had his castle, was the right one?

There was the little cottage, almost opposite the church gates. Impossible to mistake it for the much grander houses on either side. She knocked quietly on the door.

It seemed a pity to disturb the warm, somnolent peace of the street. A black cat on the windowsill eyed her warily but didn't feel it necessary to move. She heard someone moving inside. The door was opened by a little old woman who seemed no higher than Miss Garfield's shoulder. She had the bluest of blue eyes, pink cheeks with a clear, fresh

skin that a young girl would have been proud of, and white
hair drawn neatly back into a plaited coil. Miss Garfield
suddenly felt that she was too big, too fussily dressed, and
old. Older than this fresh-faced little woman in front of
her, as if her skin was old and her eyes were old and her
hair was tired and artificially waved.

'I'm looking for Mrs Moby,' she explained.

'Mrs Moby? That's me.'

It wasn't easy to explain.

'It's rather a long story,' she began hesitatingly.

'Won't you come inside?'

Mrs Moby made her way to the rocking chair where the
imprint on the knitted cushion cover showed she had sat
before. Miss Garfield sat on the sofa. The fire burned
brightly in the shiny black grate. The colours in the rag rug
gleamed on the red tiles. A grandfather clock ticked
solemnly, and the dishes on the dresser shone.

'Well,' Miss Garfield began, 'I am Headmistress of a
school in Leeds. A girl came to my school a few weeks ago,
called Anne Moby. I wondered if she might be a relative of
yours.'

Mrs Moby gazed at the fire. Then she shook her head.

'Nay. I don't think she would be,' she said.

'You haven't any grandchildren?'

'My son was killed in the army before he married. And
my brother went to America, and we're out of touch, but I
fancy his family will be grown up – the grandchildren – by
now.'

'You haven't a daughter?'

'No.'

The kindly old face changed. The soft mouth hardened,
and the blue eyes looked past Miss Garfield as if they
didn't like what they saw.

In the silence, the ticking of the clock sounded louder.

'Won't you have a drink of tea? You'll have come some way.'

Miss Garfield accepted gratefully. She sat savouring her disappointment – or rather her disappointment for Anne, and her sadness at the uncertain future she saw stretching ahead for her. If it had been different, surely Anne would have liked this bright little house, and a granny of her own? The sun through the window threw patterns on the floor; geraniums stood in pots on the sill, with a funny little cactus beside them. The cat stalked in and sat on the rug.

Mrs Moby seemed oddly unhandy, making the tea. She felt for the caddy rather than looked for it. She was a little slow arranging the cups and saucers. She was very careful in pouring the boiling water, bending down and watching carefully. Miss Garfield was too busy thinking about Anne to take much notice.

There were photographs on the mantelpiece. One of them was of a smiling young soldier. That would be the son who had been killed. One was a wedding photograph, faded and brown. That would be Mrs Moby and her husband. Rather at the back, propped against the wall, was another photograph. Miss Garfield got to her feet to look at it more closely. It was of a young girl. Dark eyes looked out boldly under level brows. Surely there was a resemblance to Anne, though the expression was so different?

'Who is this a photograph of?' she asked.

Mrs Moby paused in her tea-making but did not reply.

'I'm sorry,' Miss Garfield apologised, feeling she had been rudely inquisitive. 'It's just that this girl I was telling you about, Anne Moby, looks rather like the girl in the photograph.'

Mrs Moby poured the tea carefully into two pretty cups, and put a knitted cosy on the tea-pot.

'That was my daughter,' she said at last.

'She died too? Oh dear! I'm so sorry!'

'No.' The old lady was incapable of telling a lie. 'At least, I don't know. I heard she'd died, but no one bid me to the funeral. I don't know what became of her. She was working in a café in one of the big towns at the start. She came home and said she'd lost her job and got herself in trouble. We went to see the man, but he'd a wife and family so there wasn't much we could do about it. Ruining him wouldn't have helped my girl. She stayed here till the baby was nearly due – but it was too quiet for her. One day she just left, said she'd found a man to look after her. And I've never seen nor heard of her since. It broke her Dad's heart, losing her and Alan like that. He used to sit in that chair, smoking his pipe and not saying a word. Then he got a cold and it turned to pneumonia and he died. But really it was that he was pulled down with grieving. That's why I couldn't forgive Mary if she came home. I think of her as dead. That's what she is, to me. My neighbour read me a bit out of the paper, last year, that a Mary Moby had been killed in an accident in Huddersfield. I thought that was the end of it.'

The old mouth trembled pathetically, and Miss Garfield reached across and took her hand and held it for a moment.

'I'm sorry,' she said again. 'I wouldn't have raised unhappy memories if I'd known. But you see this girl in my school – Anne – her mother went off and left her some weeks ago. She doesn't seem to have a relative in the world. The man she called 'Dad' wasn't her real father, and anyway he's gone too. She's in the care of the authorities at present. I suppose they'll have to try and find foster parents for her, but there's no knowing . . .'

They sipped their tea. The cat lay stretched on the rug and the clock ticked slowly and patiently as if it had endless time to count and need not hurry.

'Was this girl's mother called Mary?'

'As a matter of fact she was.'

'Sounds like our Mary, to clear off like that when it suited her. And with a man and not married.'

'But Mary is a common name remember. There must be very many Marys in Yorkshire. It was just that Anne's name was Moby, and there aren't many Mobys. Anne said her mother's name sounded like an important family in the village she came from; so when I found the Mowbrays once lived here, I thought – perhaps it was – perhaps you were – her granny.'

'Our Mary was taken with the idea of the Mowbrays. Only time she took an interest in her school work was when the teacher told her about them. Fancied herself as the last of them, for a time. But they died out years and years ago. The big house at the corner is called after them, but it's got nothing to do with them. Sir Fred Moore lived there.'

Miss Garfield put down her cup and prepared to leave.

'I wish I could see this girl,' said Mrs Moby. 'Maybe I'd have an idea then of whether or not she's our'n. I don't like to think of our grandchild left like that. But it's a big thing to take on a bairn at my age. I don't know . . .'

'I could bring Anne tomorrow, if you'd like to see her.'

Mrs Moby hesitated.

'Yes,' she said at last. 'I think I ought to see her. But I can't promise anything! I don't know how we'd know. I wish I'd Albert to ask . . .'

'Don't worry,' said Miss Garfield reassuringly. 'If you decide to do nothing Anne will be no worse off than before. No one will rush you into deciding. I'll bring Anne, and then you can see . . .'

Miss Garfield did not hurry back. She spent the rest of the day wondering if she had done the right thing. Who was she to play God and arrange people's lives? Suppose it wasn't the same family, and Anne had to face another disappointment and rejection? Suppose the old lady thought it was right and took Anne – Anne had a bad record. She had been good lately, but her record really was shocking. Theft as well as truancy. Would she be bringing trouble into the evening of that dear old lady's life, when she had had so much trouble already? But now it seemed possible this was the granny, had she the right to keep quiet and rob Anne of perhaps the last chance of being with her own family?

In the end she decided to leave it to providence. She would take Anne tomorrow, and see what happened.

It was dusk when Miss Garfield reached the city. She went straight to the hostel. Anne wasn't eating her supper with the other girls. She was locked in a room by herself.

She had taken money from the Warden's handbag and spent it on fish-and-chips and going to the pictures. She had admitted it when she returned an hour ago.

'Oh dear!' said Miss Garfield, all her plans suddenly shattered. 'Oh DEAR!'

Chapter 5

Miss Garfield was taken to see Anne.

The punishment room had been a small pantry. There were bare shelves, a brick floor, a bare electric light bulb high overhead and a broken-backed chair. Miss Garfield stood inside the room and looked at Anne accusingly.

Anne rose from the chair and stood awkwardly, not knowing what to do with her hands. She raised one to her face and began to chew her already bitten finger nails.

'Don't do that, Anne! Is it true what they say you've done today?'

Anne looked at Miss Garfield's comfortable tweeds and then at her face, flushed from a day in the spring sunshine.

Well, she's had a good day anyway, she thought. Didn't have to nick the money for her petrol neither, I bet.

Among all her troubles, Miss Garfield almost merged into 'Them'.

'They say you took money from the Warden's purse.'

'Yes.'

'You did?'

'Yes.'

'Why?'

'I wanted some fish-an'-chips. Haven't had none for weeks. And I wanted to go to the pictures. It was the new Superman.'

Miss Garfield wished there was somewhere to sit down.

How could you sort out a child's outlook on life standing in a disused pantry six feet by four?

The latch lifted and John Lambert came in.

'Sorry it took so long for them to find me. I've been out with a youth club all day.' There was barely room for all three of them to stand. 'Let's get out of here – I think the kitchen's empty.'

The kitchen smelt of stale food and gas, and a tap was dripping. They sat round a formica covered table.

Anne was still and silent.

The white strip-lighting made them all look gaunt and colourless. The smell of gas and detergent was sickening.

'Well, the Warden's not prepared to keep you here now, so I suppose it will have to be Bedford Row,' John Lambert said sadly. 'And Court next week.'

This caught Anne's attention. Court? Prison? There was something worse than 'in Care' then? She wished she'd known. Why hadn't Ma told her?

She was taken to collect her belongings. Miss Garfield saw her coming back along the corridor, plastic bag in one hand, newspaper parcel under her arm, just as before, except that her clothes were cleaner and she wore socks now.

John Lambert took Miss Garfield and Anne outside, holding Anne's arm firmly. The police had had enough trouble with her already, without having to chase her and search for her again.

'I suggest Anne comes home with me for the night while we think about her case,' said Miss Garfield.

John Lambert looked at her quizzically. He suspected that she had qualms about her generous offer, and that it stemmed from compassion rather than commonsense. She guessed what he was thinking, and was afraid it might be true.

'Oh! Come on!' she cried impatiently. 'I've been out all day and I want to get home. Come along both of you – it's only five minutes' drive – and we can sit comfortably and talk. Will you bring Anne? And follow my car.'

So they set off, John Lambert wondering what he would do if Anne made a bolt for it when they stopped at the traffic lights. He had fastened her seat belt and locked the door on the inside, but she was a quick-witted kid and fast as greased lightning, he'd bet.

Anne did think of it, but it didn't seem a brilliant idea. Where would she sleep? The days on her own had made her realise you have to eat fairly often, and you need money to do that. Besides, it would be interesting to see where Miss Garfield lived, even if it was a bit alarming.

When they arrived, the house was certainly not up to Hollywood standards; but it was a comfortable and well-kept little bungalow and the cat was delighted to see her back and came forward to say so. Inside it was warm and clean and there were so many things – books and pictures and cushions – and flowers of course. Miss Garfield disappeared into the kitchen to make coffee.

'You'll need this,' she said, pouring out a cup for John Lambert. 'It must have been a long day.'

He looked at his watch.

'Thirteen hours so far.'

'It's no use,' he said, leaning back. 'Anne, why in the world did you take that money? You must have known they'd find out.'

Anne put her cup down carefully. She had been drinking so delicately, feeling every inch a lady – and now her illusion was shattered like pieces of coloured glass. She remained silent. How could she explain?

'You see, you wanted the money to buy things – but the Warden wanted the money too, and it was *hers*.'

'But she had some more money, and I hadn't any.'

'If I'd only taken Anne with me today!' Miss Garfield said.

'It's no use hoping someone will take Anne out all the time to prevent her stealing,' John Lambert said, more sternly than he'd spoken previously. 'She's got to learn how to manage without breaking the law.'

'What will happen to her?'

'Well – Bedford Row for now. It's a sort of Borstal. And Court next week. Probation I'd think at her age. But they won't have her back at the hostel and the word will get round and it won't be easy to get her in another – we're short of places anyway. That'll mean Bedford Row or somewhere like it indefinitely. And the trouble is she'll meet those worse than herself there.'

'That's your problem,' said Miss Garfield. 'I've a problem too. I was thinking that perhaps I'd found Anne's granny.'

Who would have thought that the plain, sullen, thin little face could suddenly glow with life and the eyes light up so?

'My granny?' she asked breathlessly.

'Don't count on it, Anne. It may not be her at all. But her name is Moby and she once had a daughter called Mary, like your mother's called.'

She went on to explain how she had spent the day.

'So I promised to take Anne tomorrow. And now this happens. Of course, she may say she doesn't think Anne is her granddaughter; or that she's thought again and doesn't want the responsibility. But it isn't that that worries me at the moment – you took what you wanted, Anne, and didn't bother about anyone else, so it doesn't seem so hard if the world treats you the same way and doesn't bother about you. It worries me more to think of you with that kind old lady when she's had so much trouble already, if you're likely to do this sort of thing. Can I risk her peace of mind for you, even if Mr Lambert could fix it with the authorities?'

Anne didn't say anything for a minute or two, while the others waited and considered.

'That's fair,' she said suddenly.

'What do you mean?'

'She's had her troubles. It's not fair to ask her to take on more trouble. She might not have the money, either.'

'Would you like to go if she'd have you?'

'Yes!'

'In the country? No cinema? Probably no fish-and-chips either?'

'I don't know. I wasn't ever in the country. I'd like to live in a proper house.'

'I'd probably be able to get this Mrs Moby an allowance, as far as the money is concerned.'

Anne wouldn't beg, but she held her breath in hope.

'Well, we'll have to see,' Miss Garfield said at last. 'I'll take Anne to see Mrs Moby tomorrow. We'll know better after that. You must go now – you look tired out . . .'

She helped John Lambert into his coat and saw him to the front door.

Anne heard their footsteps retreating down the hall. She dropped down on the hearthrug and clutched the huge ginger cat to her skinny chest – to his great surprise, though he accepted it politely.

'Please!' she whispered into his whiskers. 'Please! Please!'

Miss Garfield came back and was touched by the child's overwhelming affection for old Tommy. How much she must want love and 'belonging'!

She collected up the coffee cups, bathed Anne and washed her hair, and put her to bed between primrose yellow nylon sheets. Anne thought it was like sleeping at the Hilton Hotel.

Chapter 6

Anne had never had a meal like breakfast next morning. They ate in a little breakfast room, because it caught the early sunshine. There was a small posy of spring flowers on the table, and mats with pictures of birds on. There was a little pot of marmalade and a thing to put the toast in – and it was little slices that just fit. The china had flowers on, and the colours matched the cloth that was folded in her place. She unfolded that reverently and put it on her knee, copying Miss Garfield.

It was a shame that she couldn't eat more when there were so many things laid out – but she was overcome by the importance of the dishes. Which knife to use? Which spoon for the egg? Coffee to drink! Real coffee, not instant. It was splendid but rather uncomfortable, and she was glad when the meal was over.

Then there was clearing the table. The telephone called Miss Garfield away, and Anne wondered what she should do. She was so afraid – she, who never admitted she feared anything! – of upsetting a drop of coffee on the table, or spilling crumbs, or, dreadful thought, dropping some of the china and breaking it! So she did nothing until Miss Garfield came back.

'That was John Lambert,' she said briskly. 'He wants to come with us, so I said he certainly could. A day in the country will do him good.'

Wonder if it's to see I don't run off? Anne thought.

It was another fine day. Anne was put in the back because John Lambert's legs were too long to fit in there comfortably. He was glad that they wouldn't have to worry what Anne was up to if she was safely tucked in behind – it was a two-door car. And Anne was glad not to have to talk to 'Them' on the way. As it was she could enjoy the journey. She had almost never been outside the towns where she had lived; the last houses gave way to fields, hedgerows laden with white blossom, trees in palest green new coverings – so much to see, so many different sorts of houses and cars and shops and churches. So much world of a new sort, and years and years for her to find it out and live in it. She didn't take any notice of what the two in front said; and they, finding she seemed content, enjoyed each other's company in peace . . . until they left a small town and the road became narrower.

'Not far now, Anne,' said Miss Garfield, talking over her shoulder. 'We'll be at the village in about a quarter of an hour.'

Anne experienced a funny feeling in her inside. Did she want this to work out or not? It was all right to see all this country, but how did you live in a place like this? She wouldn't know anything about it. And this 'granny'? It wouldn't be like Ma. She somehow knew that 'granny' wouldn't smoke all the time like Ma, or use those sort of words, or not wash her face first thing in the morning, or be easy and comfortable while they ate fish-and-chips out of paper, watching a film on telly. It'd be more like the way Miss Garfield lived, she bet. A chilly feeling wriggled down her spine. She even felt a bit weepy.

I want Ma! she couldn't help thinking.

The car drew up opposite the gate to a church. It was half past eleven and people were coming out, walking down the gravel path in little groups, standing to chat in the sunshine. Anne felt stiff as she scrambled out of the back of the car.

'Come along, Anne.'

Miss Garfield led the way; John Lambert brought up the rear. The people talking on the opposite pavement looked with curiosity to see so many visitors for old Mrs Moby.

Then the door opened. Anne was half shielded by Miss Garfield, but she could see this Mrs Moby all right. She was amazed how small she was! And how neat and clean. How old. And not in any way at all like Ma.

Mrs Moby could only see half of Anne; half of a thin, white face; half of a mop of dark, rather wild hair; one skinny leg; and one dark eye. Then Miss Garfield drew Anne forward, and Mrs Moby peered more closely. So small! Such delicate features and hands. Her daughter had been dark, but she had been highly-coloured, pink and black and white – this child was all black and white. Not in the very least like their Mary.

'Come in,' she said.

Mr Lambert was introduced, they were all seated, tea was made and there were buttered scones to go with it.

What a marvellous place, thought John Lambert. But he feared it was not for Anne. Instinct told him that nothing in her background could be part of this other sort of life. Miss Garfield still pinned her faith on that photograph on the mantelpiece. She took it now and showed it to Anne.

'Is that like your mother?'

Anne looked closely at the old snapshot. Whoever it was had only been about fifteen when it was taken. Her mother had always been quite old, quite grown-up. She couldn't think what she might have been like as a girl.

'I don't know,' was all she could say.

46

'It's no use asking questions about what Anne remembers, because her mother didn't talk about her old home,' said Miss Garfield, replacing the photograph on the mantelpiece. 'I really don't know how we can find out . . . Does she remind you of your daughter?' she asked.

'Well – she's dark like our Mary . . . But Mary was a big girl, lots of colour . . .'

'Perhaps it was the difference of living in the country and your good food?'

'It could be . . .'

The tea was drunk, the cups empty, the scones eaten.

'Well . . .' John Lambert broke the silence.

'What will happen to the lass if she goes back to Leeds?'

They felt some detailed explanations were due, but it was difficult to talk about Anne's record in front of her. But they couldn't very well send her out to the car or into the street.

'Mrs Moby,' John Lambert said straightforwardly, 'I don't know how much you know about the position. Anne has moved from place to place, from school to school – and her mother seems to have introduced at least one man as 'Dad' who wasn't Anne's father – he is dead, she says. So perhaps it isn't surprising that she hasn't always acted as you would like your granddaughter to behave. In fact she's had to leave one or two schools; and at the moment she's in trouble with the police because she took some money from the hostel where she's been staying. If she goes back, she'll have to go to another hostel, a stricter one, for children on probation – unless we can find foster parents for her. She doesn't like hostels, and I wish she didn't have to go to one. I think she'd be much better in a home of her own.

'Now, she *may* be your granddaughter, and if so, you

won't want her with strangers and out of your care. Or she may not. In the circumstances, as a rule you would not be acceptable as a foster parent, because you are on your own; and because, if you don't mind my saying so, you are not as young as you were. But if it seems likely that you *are* Anne's grandmother, I think I could arrange it that you got paid as if you were a foster parent, and had that sort of responsibility, until we get news of Anne's mother – which we probably will, sooner or later. It is for you to decide – and Anne too, to some extent . . . You can either say definitely now, "No, I know she's not my daughter's child," and that's an end of it; or you can say, "Yes, I'm sure she is" – but I don't think you're ready to say that? Or you can say, "I don't know but I think it's likely enough for me to try keeping her for now." '

Mrs Moby looked confused. Albert had always taken the decisions. What would he want her to do now? She looked across at the chair where he used to sit. He had never been a man of many words, but she knew how he felt about things.

He wouldn't have wanted any relative of theirs in one of those hostels. She was sure.

Anne was sitting on a stool beside her, and the old lady turned to look at her closely. The hair was thicker and stronger than their Mary's, with no hint of brown in it. Anne looked up at her. The eyes were dark and deep, not bold like Mary's had been. She felt no kinship, no sense of familiarity, and she was on the point of saying so; but her attention was caught by the frailty of the face, its small, pale outline, and resolute look, although the child seemed to be holding her lips together with an effort.

Miss Garfield broke the silence.

'Would you like to live here, Anne?'

48

It was better than a hostel! And Ma would know where to find her. And the old woman didn't look as if she'd be difficult to manage with.

'Yes, Miss Garfield,' she said.

A decision had to be made.

I can't say no, the old lady thought wildly. I can't send the child back to strangers in that town. I wouldn't send old Sammy there!

'Suppose it doesn't work out properly and I can't manage?'

'We'll keep in touch – both Miss Garfield and I. And we'll come and see you at once if there's trouble. And if you find you can't manage, or that Anne isn't a relative, we'll take her away.'

'I'd like to try, anyway,' Mrs Moby said slowly.

Anne glanced at her admiringly.

That's brave of her, she thought, to take on someone like me at her age.

'And you, Anne?'

'I'd like to try it too,' she said.

No use urging her to be good, and to be grateful and to think of the old lady and what she's doing for her, thought Miss Garfield. It never is.

'Well – we'll take Anne back, and she can stay with me for now. And we'll bring her in a few days when the formalities are sorted out.'

She got to her feet, and held Mrs Moby's hands warmly.

'Don't worry,' she said. 'I'll come and see Anne often, and help you in any way I can.'

Then they were at the door, out in the spring sunshine, taking a last look back at the little cottage and the little old lady standing in the doorway, shading her eyes from the sun.

She's no daughter of our Mary's, thought Mrs Moby, noting the light grace with which Anne walked.

She's not Ma's mother, thought Anne, noting how small Mrs Moby was and how good and 'proper'.

Neither said a word. They waved, and the car drove away.

Chapter 7

A week later, Anne was installed at Rose Cottage with old Mrs Moby. It was a cool, rainy evening, and as the sound of Miss Garfield's car died away and the door was shut, all the people concerned felt rather exhausted and apprehensive. Miss Garfield still wished she had not been so responsible for something of such dubious success. Anne looked at the quiet street, and round the quiet house and wondered what she could do to pass the time here – and besides, it had always ended badly before, this would too, probably, whatever she meant to try and do – and now she had lost her place at Miss Garfield's school as well.

Old Mrs Moby was the most confused. Happy memories of when she had had children of her own in the house were revived. Living by herself had been tranquil and comfortable – but somehow not quite real. Now she felt in the mainstream of life again; but at the same time she flinched from memories of her daughter, how cruel she had been, how Albert had been hurt ... And this was her daughter's daughter, if she was anything but an illegitimate town child ...

Mrs Moby had her own deep and private worry too; but she worked so hard at keeping that to herself that she hardly considered it. Busy with their own affairs Miss Garfield and Anne had not the slightest suspicion of it.

At least the Court case was behind Anne. Miss Garfield

had made up the money she had taken, and explained that a new home had been found for her. They had jawed about 'right' and 'wrong' and 'duty to Miss Garfield who had done so much for her' until only the memory of Tommy the cat and the lemon-coloured sheets stopped her feeling rather sick at the thought of Miss Garfield's everlasting goodness. Now, as the quiet evening settled down and she had time to think, she remembered how she had been brought all the way here in Miss Garfield's car, and how nothing had been said by way of 'jawing' for the whole journey. They had talked of places Miss Garfield knew – smashing places to go to some of them sounded – and all sorts of things. And she always smelt nice, all fresh and slightly fragrant. It wasn't her fault if that other lot made her seem one of 'Them'. She wasn't really. In fact one day perhaps Anne would manage to do something really clever, or get some money somehow and buy something really nice and give it to her to show . . .

'I expect you can wash dishes, Anne?'

'Yes, Mrs Moby.'

'You'd best call me Gran, I suppose.'

It meant washing up in a bowl in a brown stone sink, but the water was nice and warm. She was very careful. Then she was shown where everything went. At first Mrs Moby watched rather anxiously, but when she was satisfied that Anne could manage she used the time to bring in sticks and coal ready to light the fire in the morning. Then she put food down for Sammy, switched on the light, and took out her knitting. She usually went to church on Sunday evening, but she didn't feel up to taking Anne and explaining to everyone after such an eventful day. She switched the radio on and settled down in her favourite rocking chair.

No telly! Anne thought indignantly. Thought everyone

had a telly! What am I supposed to do?

She sat on the mat and stroked Sammy, and found herself listening to the radio play. It wasn't bad when you got used to not having pictures. When it was over, Mrs Moby took out a pack of cards.

'I always have a game of Patience before I go to bed,' she explained rather shyly.

Anne did not know how to play, but she soon picked up the idea. She was surprised when the old lady missed an obvious red eight on a dark nine.

'Won't that go there?' she pointed out.

Mrs Moby peered at the cards.

'Yes indeed. Thank you. I didn't see that.'

Anne watched carefully after that and was able to help twice more. In the end it wouldn't quite go out. Mrs Moby looked tempted to alter the order of the cards a little, but with Anne looking, she didn't like to. She gathered the pack together with a sigh and put it away.

'I always feel I'll have a better night if it comes out,' she confessed.

Then she began folding a newspaper in an odd zig-zag way.

'What's that for?'

'Firelighters. It saves sticks.'

These were carefully put to one side ready for morning.

'You'd best be going to bed.'

'But it's only nine o'clock!'

'Only nine o'clock? We went to bed at sundown when I was your age. It will be morning soon enough.'

So Anne washed her face in the downstairs bathroom, and made her way to what was to be her own room. There was a nice little bed with a flowered quilt, and the new pyjamas. She had a suitcase now and had been given a whole lot of new clothes.

She laid out her things for school next day. Blue skirt, white blouse, grey pullover, grey socks, black shoes.

'Have you got everything you want?' Mrs Moby asked, poking her head round the corner of the door. Anne saw with surprise that the old lady had a mug of water and a clean pair of stockings in her hand. She must be going to bed too! At nine o'clock!

'Yes, thank you,' said Anne with careful politeness.

'Goodnight then. Sleep well.'

'Goodnight.'

Anne hurried into her nightclothes and jumped into bed. It was nice to have someone say goodnight to you. It was!

I hope she sleeps quiet and doesn't go sleep-walking or anything, thought Mrs Moby as she undressed with a little difficulty because her limbs were stiff with rheumatism. Shoes and stockings seemed particularly far away.

But as she propped herself against her high pillows and resigned herself to the night, she felt happier not to be alone in the house any more.

The village school was less than a hundred yards down the hill from Rose Cottage. Anne felt silly being taken along by her Gran, and silly in her strange new clothes. They weren't her sort of thing, but it didn't seem possible to avoid them. She'd have felt better able to face the world in her jeans. And it was only giving people the wrong idea to let them see her like this.

There was no problem about enrolment; Miss Garfield had left a slip of paper with all the necessary details. There was nothing to do but stand around in the playground and wait for school to start.

There were about equal numbers of boys and girls; and all ages from infants to, she supposed, about her own age – nearly eleven. Some of the girls were skipping and the others running in and out of the rope as the words told them to. The biggest boys were playing marbles. One of them, George, was especially good at it and kept swooping up a handful he'd won until his pocket was bulging. The others were ready to give up in disgust when the Headmaster came out and rang a handbell and they all trooped into school.

Anne weighed up her surroundings. The school was more cheerful than most she'd been to – probably because the doors were left open, and the windows were open, and a tank of small wriggly creatures stood on the back window-sill, and wild flowers – they must be wild flowers, they didn't look like anything she'd seen in gardens or the shops – were on the other window-sills. But the floor was only wooden planks; and when assembly was over, the big boys hauled a screen across to separate the two rooms; and you could still hear what the Infants were doing.

The Headmaster was taking dinner money, and they were told to get on with their nature diaries. Anne was given a nice new drawing book for this, but she had nothing to put in it of course. Would it be called cheating if she looked at what her neighbour, Jenny, was doing?

Jenny was drawing a twig with leaves and flowers on it.

'What's that?' Anne whispered.

Jenny pointed to the sprig she'd brought with her and put beside her book.

'Hawthorn,' she said. 'The first I've seen out.'

Anne had never seen it before in her life. Jenny gave it to her to look at. The scent was very strong. She found it had sharp thorns when one pricked her finger. She looked suspiciously at Jenny to see if she'd done it on purpose, but

Jenny looked so innocent and surprised that she decided not. Jenny must have thought she'd know the thing had thorns! She wanted to find out where she'd got it, and how she'd got it, was it hers or did it belong to someone else, was it out of someone's garden. But she didn't like to admit her ignorance. Jenny took the sprig back and went on with her drawing. Anne watched admiringly. Then she turned to her own book and wrote her name on the cover in the best writing she could manage.

Mr Hulme, the Headmaster, raised his eyes from the queue paying their dinner money and realised that Anne had nothing to do.

'You can take something from one of the jars on the window-sill, Anne Moby,' he said, and returned to his accounts.

The others turned to look at her. Most of them didn't know who she was, but they knew old Mrs Moby.

Anne wriggled out of her desk and made her way to the window-sill. The room was very crowded – more even than the rooms had been at Miss Garfield's school.

One of the oldest looking girls was putting fresh water in the jam-jars and arranging the new flowers and grasses that had been brought.

'Which would you like?' she asked.

Anne didn't know the names of any of them.

'That one,' she said, pointing to the biggest and yellowest.

The girl disentangled it and gave it to her. She took it to her desk and tried to draw it. She wished she could, it looked so splendid and rich, deep golden with shiny deep green leaves. She glanced at Jenny's drawing and saw it was really lovely, neat and delicate and just like the twig. She rubbed out her own effort.

'Right!' said Mr Hulme, closing his ledger. 'Put those

things away and get out your sum books.'

'I'll take yours,' said Jenny. Anne saw her carefully tucking the two plants into a jar, making sure the stems touched water.

They're only wild flowers! she thought. You'd think they was bought!

But at the same time she was glad that Jenny's fragrant twig wasn't left to die, even if it had pricked her. Or the golden one.

She was given a new sum book to work from and one to do her sums in. She wrote her name again. She saw she had *Book Three*. Jenny had the same one. And the first page was easy, addings up. She felt pleased with herself until she went up to the front to sharpen her pencil and saw the cover of the book belonging to a girl smaller than herself. *Book Five*, it said.

So they knew she was a dunce! Despite her fine clothes! In resentment she almost stopped work. She'd show them! Like she had before!

Then Jenny smiled at her. She was ever so pretty was Jenny, with soft mousy shiny hair and grey eyes and a lovely pink and white skin and she smiled as if she really liked you. And Jenny was only on *Book Three*. A quick, skilful glance sideways showed Jenny had only done two sums and one of them was wrong.

Anne pointed with a quick finger.

'That's wrong!'

Jenny looked rueful and without any hesitation rubbed out her answer. Then she started counting on her fingers again. Anne watched and saw it came out right that time. She nodded. Jenny smiled.

A strange idea came to Anne.

Suppose she went fast and caught the others up? Like it was a race? Miss Garfield had said her reading was very good. If you could read you could learn to do old sums, probably.

She hunched her shoulders over her work and scurried on. The figures were awful, the sums were higgledy-piggledy on the page. But she had finished all of page one when Mr Hulme announced playtime.

After the break, it was what they called PE which meant jumping and playing with balls and things. Anne was delighted to take her blouse and skirt off. She had felt hampered in such grand clothes, frightened of spoiling them in any way. Now, glad her underclothes were clean and with no holes in for once, she could let herself go. She could jump. And she could catch balls as well as any boy. They piled the blocks higher and higher, and she and George jumped the highest. Then they played catching. Jenny was a proper butter-fingers she found. When the boys realised how good Anne was they threw really hard. They'd show that show-off! Anne winced as the ball hit her bare arm when she missed it, but she ran and retrieved it and threw it back equally hard. Next time she caught it and decided to give Jenny a turn. It was a nice, soft, dropping one and Jenny caught it delightedly.

'Now – a race to finish with. George and Linda pick sides.'

Anne was sure she had done well enough to show them and would be picked one of the first.

Of course the boys were picked first. Then the best of the girls. No one called Anne's name. They even picked Jenny. Then they picked Elsie who had a deformed foot and couldn't even walk easily. Anne was one of the last two to be picked. It said as clearly as any words, 'You're an outsider.'

All the joy went. Even the sun went behind a cloud. Anne ran her fastest all the same, but she didn't care who won. She noticed they didn't say anything when Elsie was slow, in fact one of them reached out to help her back the last few steps. Of course her side lost, but they didn't blame her.

Anne put her clothes on again thoughtfully. This was different from the other schools. She'd have to learn a new set of rules.

She wished they'd let her wear her jeans. She felt she was sailing under false colours. If she'd got to make a place for herself with this new lot, she'd rather do it in her own gear, trousers, hair-pulling, bad language and the lot.

But it had been nice to find her pants and vest all whole and white and as good as anybody's.

It was a full and busy day and she felt rather deserted when it was over. The taxi collected the children from a long way away – fancy, coming to school in a proper taxi! – the others went home in families and groups of friends, and she was left to walk up the road by herself. Jenny had been picked up by the taxi, and George had gone racing and wrestling up the road with three other boys.

Gran was sitting quietly in front of the fire, and tea was on the table. Anne walked up and helped herself to a piece of cake.

'Put that down!' Gran said, rousing herself. 'You've not washed your hands yet. Nor changed your school clothes!'

Another set of rules to learn. But she was glad to get into her old, familiar jeans and T-shirt and take her socks off and wear just plimsolls. Even washing her hands felt nice in the soft, cool water. Then she sat down and enjoyed her tea.

Gran asked how she had got on.

'All right.'

'You'll be in Mr Hulme's class. Who are you sitting by?'

'Jenny.'

'Which Jenny?'

'I don't know her other name. She comes in a taxi.'

'That'll be Jenny Wright. She stays at Newlands sometimes.'

'Doesn't she live here?'

'Her granddad does. Her mother was brought up here, but she went away when she got married. She isn't well sometimes and then they come back for a bit.'

So Jenny might leave. Why was it always like that, you no sooner got somewhere and began to settle down than they changed it all again. It wasn't worth trying to get settled, really.

As soon as she had eaten all she wanted, she got up, leaving her chair pushed away from the table.

'Going to look for someone to play with,' she called, and vanished through the door before Gran could begin to protest.

'Just like her mother, thinks of no one but herself,' the old lady muttered, rising stiffly to put the chair in its place. Then she sat in her armchair again to enjoy her third cup of tea.

She saw the school cleaner go down to the school, and Mr Hulme going up to post his letters. And a couple of starlings on the footpath ... At least she thought they were starlings from the noise they made, just as she thought it was the cleaner and the Headmaster from the way they walked. But she was finding it very difficult to see far these days. Surely she could see better than that just a short time ago? It was probably just old age ...

Slowly and carefully she cleared the table and washed the dishes. Bending awkwardly, she tended the fire and got the sticks and coal for morning. She listened to the news on the radio. Then she settled quietly in her rocking chair with her knitting again, waiting for Anne to come back.

As the shadows lengthened she began to worry.

Would the child be all right? Suppose she got lost in this strange place? They said there were bogs and deep pools in Mowbray these days.

She was right to guess that Anne had gone into Mowbray. She had gone to the Cross at the corner of Church Street and seen a gang of children a bit younger than herself going off down the road. They saw her, but didn't invite her to join them, or wait for her; so she trailed behind, looking as if she didn't care. She saw where they climbed over a wall into a wood. By the time she arrived, they were running along a narrow path. She lost sight of them, so she just followed the path. She could hear their voices in the distance.

It was all very tangly. Some trees had fallen down and she had to climb over them. Briars reached across the path and scratched and tripped her. Everything was growing – it wasn't all bare and worn like the wood near the flats where they rode their bikes in Leeds. Here there were all sorts of green plants – and primroses – and white flowers she didn't know – and some that smelt like onions. It all smelt like the biggest greengrocer's shop . . . She forgot she had been following the others.

Round a bend in the path she saw a mound, almost hidden away by the trees. It always felt nice to get on the highest bit, and she pushed towards it.

Then she saw there was a stone cross. It was a bit shivery, being all alone there – no sound but the birds singing, and that strange plant smell, the crowding trees, and the old cross. She really was scared. But she dared herself to go on.

Just at the foot of the cross there was an iron grating over a hole. She knocked a loose stone and heard it drop, after a pause, into water far below. It must be a well! She glanced down into the dark depths, keeping cautiously away from the edge.

She would just touch the cross, and then she'd go back, ever so quick.

A little more light came through at the top of the hill. The evening sun shone on a square of metal fixed half-way up the stone. The sunlight made it seem safer. She stood on the bottom step of the cross and reached up to read the metal plate.

Site of
Mowbray Castle
Destroyed by order of
Henry II   1173

My!

1173! She tried to count backwards, but it was too difficult. But it was *hundreds* of years ago. It didn't look that old! But that was what it said. And the well – that would have been the Castle well – where they drew the water – when they were thirsty – and for their horses – and to wash themselves.

She sat in the patch of sunlight on the steps of the cross, hugging her knees. If she looked over her shoulder she would see them – she could almost hear the horses – and the Mowbrays – with swords and armour and velvet and fur – and ladies in long dresses . . .

A blackbird scolded her intrusion noisily from a bush and broke the spell. But she felt the people who had once lived here were not far away. They might come back.

A thrush broke into a passion of song. This was now – her and the birds and the plants and flowers and just her, it was all here.

The past and the present smudged together.

The Mowbrays. That was why Miss Garfield had brought her here, 'the name of the greatest family was like . . .' Moby. Nothing of a name. But Mowbray –

Here she sat, Anne, the last of the Mowbrays, clever and beautiful, waiting for the spell to be undone so that her ragged clothes would be turned into silks and scarlet satin . . .

She didn't know how much time passed by.

Then the sun vanished, and it was grey and cold and flies began to bite and creepy-crawly things to scutter on the stone.

She would be lost! She would never find her way back!

She hurried down the mound, emerged on a path and ran along it, stumbling over the fallen trees and briars, until the evening light shone bright like at the end of a tunnel and she was at the wall by the road again. She jumped down and ran home.

Gran was at the door.

'Is that you, Anne? I thought you were lost, or run over or something.'

This Gran was so little. Anne suddenly felt sorry for her age and frailty.

'Sorry, Gran!'

'Where've you been?'

'In that wood over there.'

'Oh – Mowbray. You want to be careful in there. It used to be a lovely place, all gardens and paths – but they sold it when Sir Fred Moore died and cut the trees down and they say the dams broke and the pools flooded and it's dangerous.'

'Was Sir Fred Moore a Mowbray?'

'Goodness me, no. He came from Bradford. There aren't any Mowbrays any more.'

Why did Anne feel so sure she was wrong? She didn't say anything, just went and washed the earth and green stuff off her hands, and watched Gran make her firelighters, and helped her get her Patience out. Gran gave her a glass of milk and a bun because she'd be hungry after being out so long.

That night Patience came out properly.

Then they said, 'Goodnight,' and went to bed.

Chapter 8

It wasn't long before Anne realised she had an enemy. Jean, the girl on *Book Five* with her sums, seemed to see Anne's arrival as a challenge. She, too, was good at jumping and catching and running – but not as good as Anne. She, too, could read – better than Anne, but not much. Anne, scurrying through maths, was near the end of *Book Three* already. It wasn't bad if you thought about it a bit – like getting a game out – like old Gran's Patience, but quicker and more fun. Her work was still desperately untidy, but it was done. Her new clothes were less ostentatious as the shoes got scuffed and she pulled a thread in her pullover. She settled in so well that a stranger would think she'd been there as long as the others.

But Jean knew she hadn't, and Jean sensed a rival. So she set to work to collect a group of girls to herself, and at playtimes they looked at Anne over their shoulders and then giggled. They had secrets they wouldn't share with her. After school they ran away and left her.

At first Anne didn't mind. She liked playing with the boys best anyway. But she found the boys here didn't play with girls, unless they were sisters and useful in some way because they could throw or run particularly well. They weren't going to have the others call out 'Norman loves Anne!' and things like that.

Jenny was outside all this. Coming by taxi, from so far

away, she wasn't really part of the village. In the dinner-hour she and Anne would wander off down the road and pick a bunch of wild flowers for the nature table. Anne came to know their names. Jack-by-the-hedge – birds' eyes – lady's smock – ground ivy – chickweed . . . Once they went into the edge of Mowbray and found golden saxifrage and wood avens. There were flower books in the class-room and Anne picked one up idly and found pictures of the ones she knew now, but they had different names – Germander Speedwell and things like that. She never got better at drawing them; but in her rather lonely evenings she took walks, looking for new ones. Jean kept the list of new finds, and if she could mislay any of Anne's 'finds' or claim she'd found the same thing herself first, she did.

This really was the only blot on the happiest bit of living Anne had ever known. Gran was kind, if a bit slow and quiet – as if she had some worry on her mind really. Was she short of money because of keeping her? She asked, but Gran said no, she got her allowance, and that it was all right. So Anne didn't know what it was, and didn't think about it much. Most of them at school were nice, too, with each other as well as with her. She thought George was the nicest – he was first in everything except work – with the fairest blond hair – and the brownest skin – and the tallest. She just worshipped George from a distance and hardly ever spoke to him because he was so important.

She found that there were two main gangs; George and the boys and Jean and the girls. Scouting round in Mow-bray, because that was where they all played almost every night – she didn't dare join the boys, and Jean told her she wasn't wanted when she tried to join the girls. But when they'd gone home, she looked where they'd been; and she found they had hide-outs. There were thick rhododendron bushes and the girls had found spaces in the middle and there were marks where they'd crouched down, and someone had put sticks together for a pretend fire, and stones as if they were dishes in a larder.

It was harder to find the boys' den – it was across a causeway through one of the marshes Gran was frightened about; and deep inside a group of yew trees. You had to crawl to get inside. There were look-out places and a bow and some arrows.

Anne was angry at being left out. She'd not done anything, not this time! She went to look at the girls' 'house' again, and in a sudden temper she swept aside all the stones and threw the fire-sticks away and threw a lot of old leaves inside.

She rather wished she hadn't, later, but it served them right!

Then she had the idea of making her own den. It would be a mixture of the other two – a 'house' where she could pretend to have parties and go to bed and a look-out where enemies could be held at bay. She spent three happy evenings searching for the right place before she found it in a sycamore tree uprooted by the wind. She could climb up the branches and look out. No one would take her by surprise! And she made herself a bow and arrows, though she couldn't make the string tight enough for them to fly far. Then she shaped herself a bed at one side. It felt hard and a bit cold when she lay down, so she went round collecting dry ferns and grass and leaves, until she could pretend it was a royal bed of softest down that she reclined on. But reclining was rather a bore after a few minutes, so she set to work to form her larder. She found clean, flat pebbles and stones in the stream for plates. She mixed up concoctions of mud and leaves as make-believe cakes – and then it was late and she had to run home.

The next evening she asked Gran for a bottle of water,

and saved a bun from her tea when Gran turned away to refill the teapot. So she had a proper feast in her 'house'. She practised with her bow and arrow, but it got no better; so she found a straight stick for a lance instead, that she could throw.

When she looked up from her 'cooking' she saw two rabbits just outside the branches of the fallen tree, busy seeking their supper and eating it. When she moved they scampered away.

And then it was home-time again.

The way back led her past the mound where the cross was. She always looked at it out of the corner of her eye and nodded her head, rather like they did in school when they came to the name Jesus Christ in Scripture. As if she was paying the Mowbrays her respects. But she didn't go and sit near the cross again. That was no part of every night's playing 'houses'. That was something different.

The next evening, scrounging round for more food for her larder, she found some wild raspberries. She put them on a leaf and was carrying them back carefully when she saw Valerie walking along the path by herself and looking very sad.

'Look what I've found,' she boasted.

'Raspberries,' said Valerie, looking no happier.

'Want some?'

Valerie hesitated and then helped herself to one or two carefully.

'What's the matter?'

'They won't let me play!'

So Anne invited her to her tree-house, and it was much more fun and between them they thought of all sorts of new things they wouldn't have thought of on their own.

As Jean's rather sharp temper turned away others, they gravitated to Anne, until she found she had a gang of her own. Sometimes some of the younger boys came too – not George and the older ones of course – but Anne's house wasn't 'cissy' like girls' houses generally were, she had look-outs and spears and things. They made the girls a better bow and arrow. They played tracking. They ambushed and raided Jean's house and took away prisoners. Sometimes, tracking each other, they came upon animal tracks. A big mound, almost like the Castle mound, was where badgers lived, they said. And a smelly hole, they thought, might be a fox's den.

It made it more scary running home at bedtime to know there were wild animals in the wood . . . Anne was always the last to go. Sometimes she was later than Gran liked through waiting to be last. But she felt so much that Mowbray was HER place, that she had to be last and alone with whoever was there – as the last blackbird called and the new moon came up through the branches. Gran thought it was just naughtiness, but she was too old and bothered to try to punish her. And in other ways Anne was a good girl – happy and friendly about the house. She never seemed to see any jobs that wanted doing, but she did what she was asked without too much trouble – except this business of coming home late.

'Why are you late again?'

'Well, Mike wouldn't go.'

'Why did you wait for him?'

'I have to be last!'

That didn't sound as if she was fooling about with boys to keep her late. Mike was only seven and the policeman's son.

'Michael ought to be in before that time.'

There were two special times. The first was a Sunday

afternoon. She wasn't playing 'houses', she was just walking and looking. The sun was very bright and warm, and
she sat down on a bank, screened by trees, to listen to the
birds – she'd never heard them sing so – and look at the
rhododendrons blooming on the bank the other side of the
stream. She heard a rustle, and thought it was a rabbit. So
she looked quite casually, because she was used to seeing
rabbits close by quite often. But it wasn't. It was a dog. And
three little dogs appeared and started to tease their
mother. But they hadn't 'appeared' – they'd come out of
that hole in the ground. They must live there. They
weren't dogs – they were FOXES. The light breeze was
blowing away from her, and the foxes could not see her.
She held her breath as she watched. But they went on
playing so long she had to breathe again.

Then she heard someone coming through the wood
behind her. She got up quickly but carefully and waved to
the intruder to be quiet.

It was George!

He looked disdainful and was not going to take any
notice.

She grabbed his arm and pointed.

George, being George, noticed and understood at once.
They stood side by side, watching. After a while they
lowered themselves carefully to the ground. The fox cubs
rolled and played, ambushed each other, worried an old
bone they found, darted at their mother who was keeping
guard – ran back into their fox-hole and out again. They
were so pretty, so clever, so strange.

And George was there, his brown hand almost touching
her own.

Then – it must have been half-an-hour or more later –
they heard the shrill voices of one of the gangs coming.
The foxes vanished.

George got to his feet, gave her a curt nod, and hurried away. She understood. Neither of them wanted it known that George had been sitting with Anne Moby in the wood.

But it had been the greatest hour of Anne's life.

The other time was one evening when it had turned wet so the others had gone home early. Anne didn't want to go home. There'd be nothing to do but play with Sammy and talk to Gran or listen to the radio – she'd finished her library book and forgotten to change it. She was wearing her oldest clothes so it didn't matter getting wet – and it wasn't hard or cold rain.

She knew what she was going to do.

She made her way to the cross.

She wasn't frightened this time. She had felt since the first time that she was accepted. No one there was going to harm her. In fact she almost felt as if the Mowbrays expected to see her again, and that she should go.

She made her way carefully and quietly, and crouched down on the lowest step of the cross. It was late in summer, and the birds didn't sing so much. There were one or two rustlings in the undergrowth, but otherwise it was very quiet. No wind. The rain pattered on the leaves; and the stream 'talked' softly at the bottom of the slope. Anne looked away through the trees.

They would have heard the stream. It would be louder when there'd been rain, just as it was now. They would have got wet – and have had to get dry – their hair would be wet and their clothes . . .

Who was it?

The Mowbrays.

But who? Which? Old or young?

It was young. It was a young man – a boy really – wearing a tunic. He ought to have a coat or a cloak or something in the rain. She knew he knew he should . . . He was somewhere behind her, and to one side. If she kept still he might come nearer.

I'm Anne! she thought fiercely. I'm Anne Mowbray. You know me because I'm a Mowbray too. You KNOW me . . .

She felt that they had known each other, once, sometime, before.

'I'm Anne . . .'

She kept the idea hard in her head, as if that was the magnet that held them together.

Then she got to her feet and bravely and slowly turned around.

Of course there was nothing there but the branches and leaves and bracken.

Then how did she know that Someone had been a bit taller than herself, and had had dark hair, and funny eyebrows that almost met in the middle of his forehead, very level and very dark . . .?

And that he'd smiled?

'But he did,' she said.

She smiled in that direction – at the trees.

Then carefully and courteously she left the cross and made her way out of the wood.

Chapter 9

It was the last day of the summer term. That meant the last day in that school for the 'top' ones. Anne and Jenny and George and Jean and William and Linda and Brian would all be leaving.

'So we'll be going to the same school, even if you're leaving and not living here any more,' Anne explained to Jenny.

They were wandering down the road in the dinner hour. Mr Hulme had said they could have an extra hour, as it was the last day. He was busy tidying cupboards ready for next term. There was no work they could do with everything put away.

'Come back at two o'clock,' he had said.

Jenny had explained that her mother was a lot better, so they must go back to Dad in Ripon.

'I don't want to go. I like it here,' she said, not exactly sadly but regretfully. Jenny never complained about things that were difficult or that she didn't like. She accepted her lot, whatever it was.

'What's been the matter with your mother?'

'She gets bad headaches and then we have to come to Granddad's.'

None of it was clear or easy to understand, but they accepted that that was how it was.

'So I shan't be able to see you in the holidays?'

'No.'

'You could come up on the bus one day.'

'I don't think mother would let me.'

'Do you think – well – I suppose we'll be able to find each other at the Comprehensive all right.'

'I don't know. They say it's ever so big.'

Anne thought of the big schools she'd been in before, but she suspected the Comprehensive was bigger than that.

'I've been in big schools,' she said. 'It'll be all right. But different.'

They walked along silently, trying to imagine the future; and then, because they knew so little about it, and finding it beyond them, they dismissed it.

They took the path through the field by the side of the wood, crossing the first stile and settling by the second, below a wild rose bush. The grass had been cropped short by sheep, but none were there now and the flowers had grown again, so the warm, dry pasture was starred with daisies and buttercups.

They began to make daisy chains, splitting the end of each stalk to thread through the next daisy head. The pink petal edgings and the freshness of the white flowers made a chain as pretty as a silversmith's work, though so fragile.

'Let's make you a queen!' Anne suggested, throwing her finished chain over Jenny's head.

So they made a crown with golden buttercups.

Then another necklace with buttercups and daisies.

Then a necklace and little crown for Anne so she could be lady-in-waiting.

The flowers felt cool and alive and a little tickly against their bare necks.

Then armlets – bracelets.

It wasn't like Anne to make someone else queen. But

Jenny was so sweet, so pretty, Mowbrays didn't seem to count. Jenny had to be the one crowned with flowers.

They stood up under the towering dog-rose bush, Jenny's soft hair starred and crowned, her simple cotton dress setting off the simplicity of the flower-jewels. She looked beautiful.

Distantly they heard a bell tinkle.

'We'll be late!'

They took off the flower chains as quickly as they could without damaging them too much, and laid them in the stream nearby. The ripples began to wash them away.

They ran back to school and arrived sun-warmed and somehow still blessed by the pollen of the flowers, just in time.

The room looked strange with all the wild flowers gone and the walls and windowsills bare. There were heaps of cast-off scrap paper piled round the waste-paper baskets. All the pencils had been collected and the library books put away. All that was left inside the desks was the little pile of used books they could take home with them.

Mr Hulme was distributing the best paintings that had been on the walls. None of them was Anne's.

Then the list of 'stars' was read out – who had the most. Jean was top of that of course.

Then the best nature diaries were handed back, and the best things in them were read out or held up and shown. John was best about birds; and Colin had painted a fabulous woodpecker – a green woodpecker. Anne had never seen one, and wondered if there really was such a thing, or if it only was to be found in some far away land. But Colin said he'd seen one, and Mr Hulme didn't say he was wrong.

One of the best books was Jenny's. There wasn't much writing, and Mr Hulme didn't mention that the spelling was funny – as Anne knew it was – but the writing was lovely, and was all somehow round the drawings so that the whole page looked like a picture. And the drawings were so like the real thing! The others clapped when it was held up and Jenny blushed very pink when she went to collect it.

I wish it was mine! Anne thought.

'Stand up.'

So this was it. They were going. Goodness knows when she'd see George again, even in the distance. Probably not till the holidays were over. Six weeks. It seemed an eternity. And Jenny was going right away. *Perhaps* to be found in a strange, big school after the holiday. And she would be going to a town school again. She realised with surprise that she hadn't really been in trouble at this school. Not bad trouble. Just once or twice . . . but no one had called her, 'THAT Anne Moby', or threatened to send her away or anything. And not because she'd been trying to be 'good', it had just happened that way. She hadn't won anything at the end, no painting, no specially good bit of work was hers – but she knew she'd been clever sometimes when they were talking; and she'd seen a gleam of approval in Mr Hulme's eye sometimes when she'd been reading. It had been good.

So she felt a sort of warm satisfaction.

And at the same time a desolate feeling because it was over for ever, it was going, almost gone – in a quarter of an hour it would be quite gone. George. Jenny. It would never be the same again.

And the threat of the big town school in the far distance. Would that mean trouble again like in Leeds? She shook the thought away. Jenny looked at her in surprise to see why she seemed to shiver when it was so warm.

They were streaming out of the door into the hot

afternoon sun. The heat came up from the asphalted playground. The light wind brought the scent of cut hay mixed with honeysuckle and wild roses. They were all laden with possessions they were taking home, all half-excited at an immensely long, unimaginably long time without school ahead; all partly disturbed at the breaking up of the familiar pattern of their lives.

Jenny turned to Anne.

'You have this,' she said shyly, afraid of offering something that perhaps wasn't worth giving, since she was so aware of her own limitations.

It was her beautiful nature diary.

There wasn't time to refuse it. Before Anne could get over her surprise Jenny had run to get in the taxi. She gave a last glance to see if Anne looked pleased with her present and when she saw her expression she waved happily out of the back window as the car drove away.

Anne wandered slowly up the road, clutching her own possessions anyhow, but holding Jenny's book as if it was a precious manuscript.

'Hello, Gran.'

'School finished?'

As always, Gran was there. As always, tea was on the table. As always, the floor was swept and clean and the dresser dusted and Sammy the cat in possession of the patch of sunlight on the hearthrug.

'Look what Jenny gave me!' Anne said proudly, dumping the other things she carried to have both hands free for the book.

She put it down in front of Gran, opening it at the drawing of a wild rose so like the real thing you could almost pick it from the page.

'Yes. Very nice,' said Gran, without sounding excited about it.

77

'Don't you think it's good?'

'Yes, I suppose so.'

Anne was puzzled. How could anyone think it was no better than that? Even Mr Hulme had praised it. Surely he'd meant it, he'd not just been saying it? She looked at the page again, and was convinced again how good it was. She saw Gran wasn't even looking at it any more.

'Come and have your tea,' said Gran, getting to her feet as Anne drew the book aside.

'Why don't you like it?'

'It's all right.'

'It's better than that!' Anne said hotly.

Gran pondered in her honest mind a minute before she admitted ruefully, 'I can't see it very well.'

'Why don't you wear your glasses then?'

'They don't do any good. Now, come and get your tea.'

A shadow seemed to creep in through the window. It was a bright afternoon, and the drawing was as clear as clear, but Gran couldn't see it, even close to. Was it just that she was old and old people didn't see so well? Would it get worse as she got older? Suppose she couldn't see well enough to manage? Well, she, Anne, would look after her! she thought fiercely. Nothing was going to happen to her Gran! In the corner of her mind 'in Care' and 'institutions' loomed and threatened. She forced them back.

It would be all right. It was just that Gran was a bit old.

But Anne hadn't the same appetite for her tea – perhaps it was a bit early with school ending so soon. And after tea she cleared the table and washed the dishes, to her Gran's surprise.

She had suddenly realised what Gran's old-ness meant. In some ways. She ought to do a bit more to help. With heavy things, like the coal.

She changed into jeans and went out to play. When she

came in at dusk she brought an armful of twigs for fire-lighting.

Gran was touched. Perhaps they'd manage after all? Perhaps nothing would get worse? At least until the lass was old enough to look after herself.

Anne put Jenny's book carefully on the little chest in her bedroom. She looked through it again before she went to bed, smiling at the funny spellings, catching her breath almost at how lovely bits of it looked.

Until she came to the wild rose page.

She shut the book quickly before she could begin to feel afraid.

Chapter 10

The holiday settled into its routine. It was a different routine from when it was school, but just as much a pattern. Gran got up and lit the fire and made breakfast. Then she settled in her chair for a leisurely last cup of tea; and Anne got in the habit of clearing the dishes and getting the coal in. Then she went out to play – in Mowbray – in the street sometimes – or on the Green where the council houses were; at some sort of tag or ball game. Or gossiping outside the fish-and-chip shop. Sometimes she ranged far and wide through the fields, where there hadn't been time to go in the evenings before. She found other woods, but none she liked as much as Mowbray. They were too much all the same, all fir trees, or all tangly and spindly trees – no grand tall trees like one or two left in Mowbray; no sense of being hand-made and people coming and going there.

One day flowed into another, and apart from the church bells on Sundays there didn't seem much difference. She and Gran went to church on Sunday evenings, dressed very proper. The service didn't mean anything to her, and she really disliked the Vicar talking on in his sermon. It wasn't her world he was talking about. No wonder more people didn't go to church. It was mostly people like Gran, who had always gone, and going was part of all their past life. She was shrewd enough to understand that.

Mr Hulme had told them that the oldest parts of the

church, the doorway and the one pillar by the pulpit, were probably part of the church Roger de Mowbray had built. The heavy ornament of the doorway fascinated her, it was so strong, each part inviting your fingers to touch, each part so freely made and all of it fitting together into such a pattern. And after all those years and years. But you couldn't look at that for long as you followed Gran in and collected your prayer book. Once you were sitting down inside, you could look and look – at the strange purple colour of the big Saxon stones at the bottom of the wall; and the simple pillar with scallops round the top that Roger de Mowbray had made to hold up the arch at the front part of his church. She didn't mind the sermon if she was looking at that. The wall slanted out of the perpendicular. Those people hadn't bothered if things weren't dead straight. Those people ... She was here with Gran, wearing her best black shoes – but those people were here too – or just outside the walls ... She thought perhaps they didn't think much of the present carry-on. But in all that long time they must have learned just to watch and not get bothered about things they didn't like.

'Now-to-God-the-Father-God-the-Son-and-God-the-Holy-Ghost-be-all-might-majesty-dominion-and-power-now-and-for-ever-Amen.'

The sermon was over and they stood for the last hymn. Gran seemed to know them all off by heart. And the prayers. She didn't use her books at all.

And then outside in the warm evening, waiting while Gran talked to this and that acquaintance; and so in, taking off Sunday clothes and getting some supper ... Another day, another week gone. How many left?

The ritual of Patience was over and Gran was putting the cards back in their box.

'Gran, how much more holiday's left?'

81

'I don't know.'

'It said on that paper when I'd to start at the Comprehensive. Where'd you put it?'

'It's on the dresser. Behind the jug.'

Anne got it and looked at it. She had got into the habit of reading anything that had to be read.

'September 14,' she said. 'What date's it now?'

'I don't know.'

'The Vicar said it was the Garden Fête on Tuesday. That's in the parish magazine.'

She looked it up and found Tuesday would be 23 August.

'Three more weeks,' she said.

She wished Gran wasn't so sad all the time, and that she'd show a bit more interest in things. It was all part of being old, she supposed.

Hope I never get old, thought Anne.

'What happened to that Miss Garfield?' Gran said suddenly, as if it was something she'd been thinking about for a long time but hadn't been sure she'd say.

'Suppose she's still being Headmistress of that school.'

'She said she'd come and see you.'

'Perhaps she will now it's holidays.'

What was all this about? Was Gran tired of having her, and wanting Miss Garfield to come and take her away? Her heart sank at the prospect. Things were going along so nicely; and in three weeks she'd be with Jenny and the others again at school.

'You tired of having me here, Gran?'

'NO!' said Gran, startled. 'No, I'm not. Not at all.' She considered for a while and went on, 'Matter of fact I'd miss you if you went now.'

She turned to collect her candlestick and cleaned some grease from it with a scrap of newspaper. Electricity or not, she liked to have a candle by her for the night.

'Then why did you ask about Miss Garfield?'

Anne looked at her shrewdly. She knew that poor, innocent Gran was quite unable to tell lies.

'Just thought I'd ask her something if she came ...' murmured Gran uneasily.

Anne went and stood in front of her.

'Gran,' she said. 'What's worrying you? Is it money? I'll try and get a job for a bit if you like.'

'No – we've got enough money,' said Gran.

'Then what is it?' Anne persisted.

Gran stood gazing at the fireplace and seemed unable to say more. Anne set her quick wits to work. If she was going to sort this out, she must know what the trouble was. Her mind raced to and fro. Not money. Not her, Anne's, behaviour, she'd not been in trouble since the holiday started.

'No one's going to turn us out of the house?'

'No – no, I don't think so,' Gran said, alarmed.

'Could they?'

'Well – perhaps they might.'

'But no one's said anything?'

'No, of course they haven't.'

It didn't sound as if it was an urgent bother then. Not money. Not having to move. Being well was the only other thing she'd ever known 'Them' troubled about. But she, Anne, was fine – skinny and not very big, but she'd never felt better. And she could run fastest in the village of the girls – and most of the boys. Gran looked all right too, with her shiny white hair and clean, clear skin – not like Ma and 'Dad' had looked in Leeds. She didn't often think of Ma these days. She tried not to.

There was one thing. Gran not being able to see so well. Was it that?

'Gran – you bothered because you can't see so well?'
There was a long silence.
'A bit.' Gran admitted. 'But I think it'll be all right.'
'What'll be all right?'
'I'll be able to manage till you leave school,' Gran blurted out. This was what had been on her mind all summer.
Anne thought about it.
'Suppose you couldn't?' she asked. 'Suppose you couldn't see well enough – I could look after things.'
'Not if you were at school, you couldn't. And I'm not sure they'd let me keep you . . . then . . .'
She means if she was BLIND! Anne thought in horror. She waited a minute to get her voice steady before she said anything.
'It may not be that bad,' she said stoutly. 'Lots of people can't see so well when they get old. You seen a doctor about it?'
'No. I didn't like to . . .'
They sat silent a while longer.
'We'd best go and see the doctor in the morning,' Anne said then. 'We've got to know where we are. He might be able to fix your eyes. Then we'd have been worrying for nothing. And it'd be nicer for you not to be bothered. We'd better go and see what he says.'
'No! I don't want to! It'll be all right. Now, you get off to bed.'
It was no use arguing. They never listened to you, they always thought they knew best. But Anne had the last word from the doorway.
'Gran, if it doesn't get better we'll go and see the doctor. While the holiday's on and I can go with you. You've not been out much lately and I'm not sure you could walk that far on your own.'

Gran knew that was true.

Sadly, they went upstairs.

Why did it have to go wrong again? Anne thought angrily. I didn't do anything wrong this time!

The other half of her mind was so sad it was crying for old Gran who could hardly see and perhaps might be . . . blind . . . one of these days.

She tossed and turned for hours as the church clock chimed through the short summer night. The first bird was stirring before she at last fell asleep.

I wish Albert was here! Gran thought, as, too tired to do more, she lay propped up with her high pillows.

Chapter 11

The very next morning the postman brought a letter. Anne was out playing, so it was laid on the dresser and she saw it when she came in for her dinner.

'Who's the letter from, Gran?'

'I don't know. I haven't read it.'

'You haven't even opened it!' Anne said accusingly, after examining it. Gran was serving out the potatoes and didn't answer.

'Shall I open it?'

'You can if you want.'

'It's from Miss Garfield!' she said, looking at the signature.

'What does it say?'

Anne read it out:

'Dear Mrs Moby,

I am sorry not to have been to see you before this, but I had a slight accident and injured my arm so I have not been able to drive the car. However, I am better now, and would like to come and see you next Friday. Do not bother to reply. If you are not at home I will call another time.

I hope you and Anne have had a pleasant summer, and am looking foward to seeing you both again.

Sincerely,

Julia Garfield.'

'Today's Wednesday,' said Anne. 'The day after tomorrow she'll be here.'

'Yes.'

'Will you be glad to see her?'

The bright blue eyes were lifted to her face – but were they as bright as they had been?

'Well, I will and I won't. I've been thinking I should tell her I don't see so well . . . But I don't want to cause trouble and have them take you away.'

'Perhaps we needn't tell her? Not this time? Not before you've seen the doctor? Perhaps we ought to go to the doctor tomorrow, before she comes, so we know . . .'

'I don't want to.'

'It's no use, Gran. You know you've got to go sooner or later. Let's not leave it till tomorrow; let's go this afternoon – there's a surgery on Wednesday afternoons, isn't there? Let's get it over!'

'I don't know . . .'

'Then we'll go. There'll be lots of time after we've done the dishes.'

It was a tasty stew, but neither of them had much appetite for it. Gran pushed her plate away after a few minutes.

'I don't seem hungry this hot weather,' she said querulously.

Anne ate doggedly. It was no use making a fuss. You had to do the things that had to be done, and missing your food and getting ill wouldn't make it any better. So she ate steadily through her meat and potatoes; and then through her rice pudding. But she was glad when it was over and she could clear the dishes away.

'I'll wash up, Gran, while you change,' she said.

'I don't know . . .'

But Anne whisked away into the back kitchen and

began to clatter the dishes. Gran sighed, and made her way to the stairs, fumbling for the bannister. Anne turned to watch her anxiously. She had taken to 'happening' to be around when Gran went upstairs, and especially when she came down, not liking the way she hesitated on the top step and peered for the next one. So now she hurried with the dishes so that she had time to run upstairs and put her school clothes on – they were getting small for her, she must be growing! – to be ready to walk down the stairs in front of Gran. It was still a bit early – only half-past one by the church clock.

They sat facing each other.

'I don't know . . .' Gran said yet again, worriedly. 'Drat my old eyes!'

'Best thing we should go,' Anne said firmly. 'Ma always went to see the doctor when she had bad headaches, and he gave her some stuff that made them better. Expect he'll say it's just you're getting a bit old, and nothing to worry about. He made Jenny's Ma better, too, and she's gone back to Ripon. Think we'd better be going now if we're going to take it easy. Bit hot for hurrying.'

She helped Gran put her hat on straight and handed her her walking stick. Then, after a slight hesitation, she took her arm. She was not used to touching people. Ma had never been one to nurse you or – anything – and not-touching had become part of her freedom and independence. But she was afraid Gran might miss her step on the cobbles or at the gate; and having started that way, they proceeded arm in arm up the street. Anne found she was as tall as Gran – and so much stronger! She marvelled at what it must feel like to have to take little steps like that, and to put one foot in front of the other so slowly. She realised that the arm linked to her own was as fragile as a bird's. It was all she could do to restrain herself from striding out and skipping and jumping along as she usually did. And how SLOW it was going on like this . . . But she did her best to make it seem ordinary.

The neighbours standing in their doorways in the afternoon sunshine were surprised to see old Mrs Moby walking up the street. It was a long time since she had been out, except to church. Where was she going? She didn't usually visit at the top end of the street.

Only past the garage and six more houses, thought Anne. We'll manage it all right.

She felt so anxious, in case the walk was too much for Gran and because of what the doctor might say.

And then they were there, in the shady, empty waiting-room. If you hadn't known what it was you'd really have known as soon as you went through the door. There was the cold smell of linoleum and wooden chairs and anti-septics, the feeling that no one lived there. And the fears and cares of the people who went there somehow lingered and met you at the door.

They were the first there. It was several minutes before a window slid back and the secretary looked through at them.

'Hello, Mrs Moby! I haven't seen you here before.'

'No, I haven't been before.'

'I don't think we have a card for you. I'd better make one out.'

All the details were taken and written down and they were so occupied that it came as a surprise when the doctor put his head round the door and said, 'Next?'

He looked puzzled, and the secretary explained that it was Mrs Moby who was seventy-one but hadn't been to the surgery since the new doctor had come to the village.

'I wish there were more like you, Mrs Moby,' the doctor exclaimed. 'It is you I'm to see, not . . .?'

'This is Anne, my – granddaughter,' said Mrs Moby, wondering if what she said was true. It seemed very important to tell the whole truth and nothing but the truth on this important occasion. She was going to add, 'Or so we think,' – but the doctor was in a hurry and held the door open for her. Anne led her towards it.

'I expect we'll manage now,' the doctor said, dismissing Anne. 'Unless you want her to come with you?'

'No,' said the brave old woman. 'I'll manage on my own now.'

She didn't want to distress Anne with any bad news before she had to.

Anne sat and frowned at a magazine, but she hadn't the slightest idea what the words said. Other people came into the surgery and a small child began to run to and fro across the floor and to shout for a book to look at – but Anne kept her head down, while thoughts whirled through her mind.

Poor Gran! Whether she was her real Gran or not, she was good, and this shouldn't happen to her! Perhaps it would be all right and they'd be walking down the street in a minute with nothing to worry about – and what a tea they'd have in celebration! Then she shivered as she realised how little Gran could really see, and how much worse she'd got this summer. Poor Gran! And what would happen to Anne herself if it was bad? The dark cloud of Leeds swirled in her head, full of institutions and Care and places they would put her, and the police.

It seemed a very long time. It must be bad if it was taking so long. At last, when the waiting-room had grown full and people were beginning to wonder impatiently who was taking so long, Mrs Moby came out. The doctor held her arm gently and led her to the secretary's window.

'No treatment,' he said. 'I want you to make an appointment for Mrs Moby to see Mr Trees the next time he is in Ripon. And we'll need the ambulance to take her there.'

Anne's heart sank. Who was Mr Trees? AMBULANCE. It was bad. Bad. The whole gentle concern, it all meant bad trouble; they were only kind when you were really in trouble. She drew her eye-brows together and frowned fiercely.

'You'll get home all right, Mrs Moby?' the doctor asked, looking at her shrewdly and carefully. 'I can run you back after surgery if you like to wait.'

'No thank you. We'll walk,' Gran said with dignity.

Anne took her arm and opened the door and led her out.

They had walked some way down the street before they spoke.

'What did he say, Gran?'

Gran did not answer at once.

'I've to see this man in Ripon. He's a specialist. They won't know till then.'

'Didn't he say what he thought?'

Again there was a silence while they walked quite a long way.

'Good afternoon!' called people who knew Mrs Moby well. They spoke cheerfully, but they looked at her curiously, because the word had gone round that old Mrs Moby had gone to see the doctor, and they wondered what it was.

'He thinks it's something with a long name – I forget what it is. But if he's right, it's got to be left to go its course. Before they operate. If that goes all right I'll be able to see better again.'

'That's not bad!' said Anne robustly. 'Lots of folk have operations. They're ever so good with them these days, aren't they?'

Mrs Moby didn't reply. She couldn't bring herself to say just yet that the doctor had said that – if he was right – there would be a time when she wouldn't be able to see at all.

And so they made their way back up the sunny street, greeted by neighbours, passing one familiar doorway and uneven bit of path after the other, until they were home, the door was unlocked, and Gran sank into her rocking chair.

'Take your hat off, Gran, and I'll put it away for you. And I'll make some tea as soon as I've changed.'

She ran upstairs and hurried to take off her best clothes and get into jeans and a shirt. She could cope better like that.

Mrs Moby rocked gently in her chair.

Bless the child! she thought. What would I do without her?

Tears pricked her eyes as she realised that she might have to do without her, if it came to the worst. She blinked them away quickly.

As they were having tea, Miss Garfield's letter caught Anne's eye.

'What are we going to tell her?' she said, nodding towards it.

'Her?'

'Miss Garfield.'

'Well – I'd like her advice. She seemed a nice lady.'

'Oh – she is. But all the same, people like that have to go by the rules and regulations Ma used to say. And she might have to do something – if she knew – or something.'

Mrs Moby understood what she meant. They might have to take Anne away and put both of them in institutions if 'They' decided they couldn't manage.

'Let's not tell her yet, Gran? Let's wait and see what this

man in Ripon says? Miss Garfield will come again now her arm's better and we could tell her then.'

Anne was crossing her fingers under the tablecloth.

'All right,' Mrs Moby agreed at last.

And so when Miss Garfield came on the Friday the talk was of her broken arm. She thought Mrs Moby looked older and more frail, but she kept her clear colouring and fresh appearance, almost like a girl . . . And Anne – she had grown; and she was thoroughly clean now as she had been thoroughly dirty before, an everyday cleanness, not a once-only cleaning up like when she'd bathed her. And she seemed to be a help to Gran, and it was good to see them together, so obviously trusting and liking each other. She found it peaceful to sit in the bright living-room again and hear the leisurely tick of the grandfather clock, and see Sammy stretched on the hearth rug and drink the fresh tea and eat the homemade scones.

'Anne made these,' Mrs Moby explained proudly.

Anne blushed. She didn't seem able to take much pride in female accomplishments like cooking and sewing and arranging her hair – she was much more proud of being the fastest runner and the best thrower – and a good reader. But now Gran found it difficult to see to cook, she had to do something.

I wonder if she really is the granddaughter? pondered Miss Garfield. Somehow I'm sure it has turned out well, whether she is or not. I must bring John Lambert and let him see that it does turn out right sometimes.

She felt reassured and happy about her visit.

'Will you be coming again?' Mrs Moby asked as she left.

Miss Garfield stopped in surprise. There seemed some anxiety behind the question.

'Would you like me to? I'd like to come if you don't mind.'

'Yes. I wish you would,' said Mrs Moby.

Anne kept her eyes on the ground.

Now what . . .? wondered Miss Garfield to herself. There's something odd here . . .

'When do you start school in Ripon, Anne?'

'In a fortnight.'

'I'll come and see you soon after that, and see if you like it there. Goodbye! Goodbye!'

She got into her neat little car and drove away, happy with her day, apart from a slight puzzlement about those last minutes on the doorstep.

'Probably I'm only imagining trouble,' she accused herself, relishing the last of the countryside before she was back in the streets of town.

'That's a nice lady,' said Mrs Moby.

Anne nodded, and then realising Gran probably hadn't seen her gesture, said, 'Yes, ever so.'

'I wonder if she noticed?' Anne asked herself, aware of Miss Garfield's ability to know things you hadn't told her.

Chapter 12

Mrs Moby's appointment at the hospital was arranged for the very day term started at the Comprehensive. Anne offered to stay home and go with her, but Mrs Moby wouldn't have it.

'No,' she said. 'You've got to make a good start. It wouldn't do to be off the very first day. All sorts of things you'd never understand after, perhaps. I'll be all right. The ambulance will pick me up at the door and bring me back. I'll leave the key under the mat in case I'm not back when you get home.'

It was a mixed sort of day for Anne – getting into school clothes again. She hadn't liked to say anything to Gran, but really what she'd worn at the village school had got skimpy – the skirt was way above her knees, and she could only just fasten it. And there was a thread drawn in the sweater. Gran seemed to have forgotten the letter said she ought to have a blazer. And the elastic in her pants was slack and not very safe. At least it was warm enough not to need a vest. Her toes were out of her plimsolls after a summer of running about in them.

Oh well, she thought, collecting her belongings and her bus pass and her old pencil case together. If they don't like it, they'll have to do the other thing.

It was fun to meet all the others on the bus. George looked wonderful – he'd grown too, and in his long grey pants and blazer he looked a smasher. The summer on the farm had bronzed his face and bleached his hair. Anne's heart missed a beat as the bus stopped to pick him up, and he sprang inside and passed up the aisle to his friends at the back.

Then the school – shivery memories of the big schools before, and the old, familiar stuffiness and smells; the loud electric bell. The assembly in the big hall. She'd not been in such a big room since she'd left Leeds. Then the classroom – just like Leeds but newer, with bigger windows – but the same sort of blackboard, and pin-up boards, and the same sort of desks and chairs. She slung her shoe bag on her chair and looked round. George was here! In her class! She'd see him again every day.

But Jenny wasn't.

It was only at playtime that she found Jenny, with difficulty, out in the noisy playground. The clipped grass seemed to stretch for ever. There were a few trees, in lines, of the ornamental sort. It was a lot better than Leeds. But not like the Kirkeby school that had seemed to grow out of its place . . . And there, standing in a corner between two walls, as if they would shield her from the crowds, was Jenny.

They hadn't much to say to each other. Just a quick look to see how like and how different from what they remembered. And a minute later the loud electric bell went and they had to find their way indoors again.

'What class are you in?' Anne asked.

'One T.'

They'd this system of giving all sorts of letters to classes, so you wouldn't know who was in the top and who was in the bottom; but it was daft because the ones from last year knew all right and they told them. Everyone knew. T was bottom. Anne and George were in J. That was next to the top.

Anne watched Jenny drift away, and hoped she'd find the right room.

It was a muddled day, full of filling in forms, taking out books and writing names in them, listening to lists of rules. The best part was PE in a smashing gym with all sorts of ropes and things to jump over and bars to walk on and work on just like the gymnastics on telly.

'Well done there,' called the teacher to her, and she glowed.

Jenny had been at a different sitting at lunch, and she hadn't managed to find her afterwards. Between one thing and another it was four o'clock before she had time to think of anything but school. Then, as they waited for the bus, she remembered the ambulance and Gran.

Expect it's all right! she thought hopefully. Here, with everything so organised and arranged it didn't seem likely or possible that something could come out of nowhere and smash all her plans. It had all been arranged that she'd come to this school and be in Class J; and no muddly thing like luck or God would interfere with that.

She felt less sure as she got off the bus and walked down Church Street home. The door was open, so Gran was back. Tea was on the table. Just as it used to be.

'Hello, Gran! How did you get on?'

'Not too bad.'

Gran had had time to think of what she was going to say.

'What did they say?'

'I've to go and have an operation on 18 November. In Harrogate.'

'Then you'll be better.'

'Probably.'

What they had really explained so kindly was that there was a half-and-half chance she'd be better.

'So you've just got to wait till then? All be over by Christmas, won't it?'

Gran turned to make the tea. She had decided there was no point in worrying the child by explaining they'd said that in a few weeks she'd not be able to see at all; and there would be a time after that before they could operate. Something might happen. No use worrying the child the first day in a new school.

'How's the new school?'

'Not bad. I saw Jenny, but she's not in my class. I'm in J. She's in T. J's next to the top.'

'What does T mean?'

'That's at the bottom,' Anne admitted.

Mrs Moby shook her head. 'Her mother never was any good at school work,' she said.

'But Jenny can draw marvellous flowers and things. And she knows all about them too.'

'Who else is in your class?'

'George Moore.'

'They're clever, those Moores. They've got on well. But they were always better at games and things – they don't like their books much.'

And so they chatted on through tea; and when it was over and Anne had done her jobs – there was no homework this first night – she took herself into Mowbray to think out her problems.

Clothes. She was going to need some new ones. She'd got used to looking tidy and even Jenny had a new skirt and jumper. Could she get a job? She knew Gran got her pension, because she cashed it for her at the post office every week, putting it into her hand and watching her count the notes and the change and stow it all carefully in her purse. And there was the other money they let Gran have for keeping her – that came as a cheque and Gran had to sign it and that money was put away in a tin in the bottom drawer under the spare table cloths. When the tin got full Gran either spent it or put it away somewhere else – the number of notes just went down from time to time. Probably that was for rent and things. Ma had always had bills – big, impossible bills. Probably Gran had the same. Perhaps there wasn't money for new clothes. Gran never seemed to have anything new and she always looked as neat as a new pin – but then she didn't grow out of things or go walking through the woods. She couldn't bother Gran now when she had this other trouble. And clothes would mean a trip to a town to buy them, and Gran couldn't manage that, could she?

Anne sat at the base of the cross in the middle of the wood, thinking. She wrinkled her nose as the problem seemed to get harder the more she thought.

And then the hospital. It was all right Gran making it sound so simple, but her eyes had got a lot worse through the summer. If they got worse again, would she be able to see enough to manage while Anne was at school? And if they got help in they'd have to admit what was happening, and 'They' might decide an old lady and a girl her age who perhaps wasn't a relative at all, couldn't manage.

The stream murmured softly as it trickled between the stones at the base of the mound. The mossy stones she sat on weren't that old, but the rim of the well – had Roger de Mowbray sat by it some evening? But it would have been inside the castle yard then, tidy and paved and clean and dry. She left the mound and moved down to the stream. That would have been the same – a bit smaller perhaps, but the same clear, brown water, stones – a thrush singing – trees overhanging. Did Roger de Mowbray have problems too? Bet he was never short of a skirt and a couple of pairs of pants! They were small things, after all. There was all this, and it was peaceful and beautiful. The clipped lawns of Ripon and the plastic classrooms and the noisy bus they went in suddenly seemed in some other and less important world.

Roger de Mowbray led his men at the Battle of the Standard. And he went twice to Jerusalem on a Crusade and slew a giant Moor in single combat. And he built the church door. 'If I'm a Mowbray, I'll be able to manage too,' Anne decided.

She loitered back through the twilight. The days were drawing in and there was a nip in the air. The thrush still sang with heart and soul – she could see him on the tip-top of a silver birch tree. The smells of earth mould and leaves soothed her; a cluster of red berries, caught in the rays of the setting sun as they struck through the branches, rewarded her.

But she'd better hurry back to Gran now, she'd been out a long time.

Gran was sitting peacefully listening to her radio. The world seemed safe and right after all.

At least it was all right until next morning, when it was raining, and her blue mac had grown so small she couldn't button it properly and it looked daft; and she hadn't a school beret. So her hair got wet and she got to school looking bedraggled and untidy. They were given a list of things they had to have – a ruler, a protractor, a set square, coloured crayons, a box to keep them in, shoes to change into indoors –

Anne muttered one of the words she hadn't used for weeks, under her breath. How was she going to get all that?

The problem was on her mind all day. No wonder they

thought she wasn't attending to her work!

When she got home, she asked Gran where Miss Garfield's letter was. Luckily it had been kept; and she saw with relief that it had an address at the top. When she had done her jobs, she said she would go upstairs and do her homework. Gran was rather proud of having a granddaughter at a big school with homework to do, and sat knitting happily enough in her armchair.

Anne slit a page from her exercise book as neatly as she could. Copying the style of Miss Garfield's letter, she put her address at the top, and the date.

'Dear Miss Garfield.' Then she stopped, chewing her pen. It wasn't easy to explain.

'I have started at the Comprehensive but I need more clothes and a protractor and things. I don't like to ask Gran. Can you lend me the money for them please? I will pay you back by getting a job helping with the paper round. Hoping you are well.
                              Yours sincerely,
                              Anne Moby.'

Anne knew where the envelopes were kept, and quietly took one, addressing it carefully. She had her week's pocket money not spent so she could buy a stamp in the lunch hour from the post office up the road from school. She was not sure if she was allowed to leave school in the lunch hour, but it was important, and old habits of breaking rules seemed to come back to her naturally.

So next day she posted her letter, hoping she'd done the right thing.

Miss Garfield was worried by the letter. Was the old lady

so confused that she didn't realise anything as simple as that the child needed clothes and shoes and things for her new school? It was serious, if so. For how could she be trusted to look after a problem like Anne? Or was she just mean about money? Because the allowance should be enough for clothes. But surely not! She had always seemed the soul of generosity. The only thing was to go and see. She wouldn't take John Lambert, though. She'd better find out just what was happening, first.

Anne wondered how long it would take Miss Garfield to answer; and how she would send the money. She never doubted she would send it. It was needed, and anyone that sensible would know it was needed and would see to it. How Anne would manage her shopping and account to Gran for the new clothes; how she would repay Miss Garfield; were harder problems, but less immediately urgent.

And then on Saturday morning at ten o'clock before Anne had gone off to play, the little car drew up at the door and there was Miss Garfield, plump and a bit breathless, curly grey hair and pink coat, at the gate.

Anne blushed as she went to meet her.

'I had your letter, Anne. Don't worry!' she said as she made a business of helping to close the gate, before following Anne down the garden path.

You would have thought nothing out of the way had happened, the way Miss Garfield accepted tea and a biscuit, stroked Sammy, talked about how her arm was better, talked about Anne's new school . . .

And then it all changed. With no alteration in her voice, as if it was as casual as the other things they'd spoken of, Miss Garfield said, 'Mrs Moby, I hope you won't mind, but

I've been wondering about something. Now Anne is growing, she'll want more shoes and new clothes. I wondered if you'd managed to get a school blazer? I know it isn't easy for you to get to town. Perhaps I could take you both to Ripon while I've the car here?'

'You know, I never thought of it!' said Mrs Moby, shaking her head. 'It's that long since I'd bairns of my own I'd forgot how they grow out of things. And that letter did say something about a blazer, now you mention it, didn't it, Anne?'

Anne nodded her head. She kept on doing that before she remembered she had to say it too.

'Yes, Gran,' she said.

So Gran wasn't going to tell that she hadn't noticed because she couldn't really see.

'I won't come, if you don't mind,' Mrs Moby went on. 'I find the crowds a bother in towns, now. But if you could take Anne and get her what she needs –'

'You'd better go and change, Anne, and we'll go straight-away . . .'

When Anne came down in her school clothes, Miss Garfield realised how urgent the problem was. She ushered her into the car and they drove off.

Anne had never known a shopping like it. Shoes. Plimsolls. Stockings and socks. Things to wear underneath. A new blue coat and a school beret. All the maths stuff – a ruler you could see through and a new pen and a pencil box. And a pretty dress for Sundays and tights and an anorak for playing in and new jeans and a red sweater with a high neck.

Then they went to a café.

'I told your Granny we wouldn't be back for dinner,' Miss Garfield explained. So they had an exciting sort of soup and steak and chips and chocolate cake and coffee.

Anne had grown very quiet.

'What's the matter, Anne?'

'I said I'd pay you back. But we've spent that much I don't know when I can pay all that.'

'You don't have to. Your Granny gave me some money while you were upstairs. It looks as if she isn't spending the allowance she gets for you, she's got it all stashed away there.'

'But it was more than she'd have thought you needed,' Anne said shrewdly.

'Then the rest can be an early Christmas present from me. After all, I haven't a daughter of my own to go shopping for, and it was fun. Wasn't it?'

They sipped their coffee in the quiet little café.

'There is one thing, Anne, that worries me rather.'

Anne looked up apprehensively.

'I'm surprised your Granny didn't notice you had grown out of your things. It wasn't that she begrudged buying more, she was eager to give me the money. But – how could she not notice? And why didn't you tell her?'

There was a long silence.

She could say Gran was a bit old but not to worry she was all right really. Or she could just play stupid and pretend she hadn't thought of it and didn't know.

Or she could tell the whole truth.

Was Miss Garfield to be trusted? Because it was Gran she was risking, as well as herself.

Miss Garfield knew there was a problem. Last time Anne hadn't told her when she was in trouble, when her mother had left her. Would she tell now? Had she changed that much?

It's not my problem, thought Anne. It's Gran's secret too. But I've got to look out for Gran, and Miss Garfield may be the best bet . . .

It was the pretty new dress that decided her. Anyone who gave you anything as special as that when they didn't have to must be proper. And – it wasn't right to take the dress and not tell the truth . . . She drew her dark brows together and looked at Miss Garfield straightly.

'It's because she can't see proper. We've been to the doctor and it's something wrong with her eyes, that has to be left before she can have an operation. She's been to hospital, too, in an ambulance. She's to have the operation on 18 November. But it bothers her. And she doesn't see so well.'

'Why didn't you let me know before? What a worry it must have been for you both!'

'She doesn't want to be taken into an institution or hospital or something and I don't want to be taken off her, and we thought you might say we couldn't manage if you knew.'

Miss Garfield thought about it.

'And can you manage, Anne?' she asked.

'YES! We'll manage. I can look after Gran.'

'What about school?'

Anne shrugged.

'I can manage that too. I'll catch up when Gran's better.'

'What about the day time, when you're away?'

'I do most things before I go and when I get back.'

Miss Garfield shook her head doubtfully.

But she really had no doubt about what she would do. She would help the pair of them to get by in their own way, if she possibly could.

They collected all their parcels and made their way back to the car.

'Tell your Granny you've told me, Anne. Tell her not to worry; I'll help all I can. I'm sure we'll manage.'

'Thank you, Miss Garfield,' Anne said, rather chokily.

Miss Garfield felt rather choky, too. Because if her scrappy knowledge of such things was anything to go by, rougher times were ahead when perhaps poor Gran wouldn't be able to see at all. And that operation wasn't the sure-fire thing Anne seemed to think it was, especially when the old lady was over seventy.

But if Anne could battle with the problem, it wasn't up to her, at her age, to fuss.

Chapter 13

It wasn't until it had happened that Anne realised what a relief it was not to feel she had the whole responsibility for the household on her shoulders. Miss Garfield knew now. Miss Garfield would see she didn't do anything daft. And Gran was happier too, now she knew Miss Garfield knew; as if just that made it sure that they'd manage and the operation would go all right. And Anne hadn't let herself think how much she minded being all shabby again until she felt the pleasure of being as neat as anyone or neater. She had managed to stitch tapes with her name on into her new clothes, and she hung them up in the cloakroom carefully. She could look at George again and hope he would notice her. She'd seen that he'd tried not to seem to know her and had a sort of disapproving look in his eye this term. All right for him! she thought with a rare burst of criticism towards anything he did – his parents had the biggest farm in the village and he just didn't know that you couldn't always have the sort of things he took for granted!

But now – she was as good as anyone – nothing was too difficult, everything was fun and fine, and she felt she could have run and leapt and danced.

Lessons were often a bit of a bore. Why didn't they teach you the sort of things you wanted to know?

She found Jenny at playtimes, as a rule. The first day she

wore her new clothes she caught a warm smile in Jenny's eyes.

'That's a nice skirt! New, isn't it?'

Anne twirled round to show it off, and bent to pull up her new socks and ostentatiously re-tie the lace on her new shoes. When she stood up again and looked at Jenny she was a little ashamed, because she saw nothing but admiration and pleasure. Not the tiniest bit of jealousy, although Jenny's skirt wasn't of such good material.

They walked on the trampled grass, where nothing but the odd daisy and dandelion seemed able to grow.

'I liked Kirkeby better!' said Jenny with a sigh.

'Can't you come out on Saturday? On the bus?'

Jenny's gentle, open face lit up. It's like a soft-coloured lamp lit up inside, Anne thought.

'I'd like to. I'll ask Mum tonight. It can't be this week though.'

The harsh bell shrilled and they hurried inside.

And the next lesson was PE and her toes weren't out of the front of her gym shoes any more, and she needn't worry in case the old elastic gave way in her pants. Nothing seemed difficult now! If it meant balancing on the bar she could walk and run and turn and jump on it as if it was a foot wide. If it was climbing up the rope she felt weightless, able to pull up hand over hand, pushed by her feet in the new plimsolls, first at the top, high above everyone and everything. She could even go leaping over the horse with a somersault at the end – something she'd felt a bit scared about before. It was like flying.

And Miss Davies said, 'Good!'

Miss Davies made her do it again, by herself, to show the others. And when she glanced at George on the way back he almost smiled. It was hard to keep her face straight so they wouldn't think she was swanking.

That evening, when she had changed and done her jobs and hurried through her homework, she went into Mowbray. It had been a scorcher of a day for the time of year; and now the sun was setting crimson in a clear sky. The beams through the trees caught the cloud of insects making the most of the last warmth and the last flowers. Anne swatted them out of the way and hurried to the cross.

There, as so often before, she sat to think.

Perhaps there was a reason for miserable things that happened after all – it was so wonderful when they came right again.

But she put that thought out of her mind straightaway. It wouldn't be right for old Gran to be bothered so and have to have an operation just so she could feel excited like this. And of course it wasn't all over yet . . . there WAS the operation. And the time before. But it was no use, she couldn't be thoughtful and sensible tonight. It was all too nice. It had been, all day.

And as if that wasn't enough, she heard voices – boys' voices – and the old gang from Kirkeby school appeared – William and Arthur – and George. And they didn't walk by as if she wasn't there like they used to. They stopped to talk. Not about anything much, just talk for an excuse to stop. For ages. Until it was beginning to get dark and she and they had to go.

Wonderful. Wonderful . . . that was a song. She sang tunelessly as she ran home through the deepening shadows.

Gran couldn't play Patience now, but luckily she could hear well, so she listened to the radio instead. She'd been listening to something about 'When I Was Young', and she was glad to have Anne to talk to about it.

'I remember . . .' she said.

Anne sat on the rag rug, stroking Sammy and listening, glad Gran was enjoying herself, but too wrapped up in the lovely present to care about the long ago. It grew dark and the street light shone through the window; but as Gran's eyes were bad it didn't matter. Only the chill evening breeze coming through the open door reminded Gran how long she had been talking.

'Bless me! What time is it?'

'Don't know, I'll put the light on.'

The electric light was bright and glaring. Anne shut the door.

'It's eight o'clock.'

'Deary, deary me!'

'I'll get supper, Gran,' said Anne, pushing the old lady gently back in her chair. It seemed the only way she could thank anyone for her lovely day. She made their warm milky drink, with biscuits for Gran and a bit of bread and cheese for herself. Later she made the firelighters and put the sticks ready for morning and got Gran her candle – and at last they were in their own rooms and Anne could shut her door. She slipped out of her clothes hurriedly and dived into bed.

In the dark, she re-lived her lovely day.

It was a week later when the Headmaster, at assembly, said he had something to say of special importance. An old pupil had presented a silver cup to the school. He held it up to show them and very grand it looked. This former scholar wished that young people cared more about being fit and well than they seemed to these days; so he asked if each year in the school could choose a team to represent them and devise a programme of dance and gymnastics. Whichever team did best would have their name engraved on the cup and keep it in their classroom for the year.

A buzz went round the hall, but they were called to order and dismissed. Back in their own rooms they talked about it – most of the girls thought it was silly. They didn't like PE and games, anyway. Several of the boys felt the same.

'Kids' stuff. Now if it were bike racin' or summat . . .'

But all the same, the idea of doing better than the bigger, older ones – or at least as well – when they'd been put in their place ever since term started and made to feel small, and called 'new kids' . . . As long as they personally didn't have to take part, a lot of them felt they'd like their team to do well.

'Who'll choose the team, Sir?'

'Miss Davies. She's the only one who knows all the classes in each year.'

Before the week was out the teams were chosen – or appointed, because the only choice really was whether those asked were willing to enter and work for the competition.

George was in their team. And Anne. And six others. Not Jenny. But they were to practise in the gym in the dinner hour. It was getting cold to hang about outside anyway, and the programme grew better and more exciting the more they got into it. They were good. They knew they were good. They practised every day, more than the older classes did. That was why they were good as a team, not just each one of them good. They'd certainly do as well as most of the older ones. Better!

Anne had never been so happy. The relief of being one of the best instead of always the worst; the pleasure of moving to music and feeling her body respond perfectly to what she wanted it to do, as if it loved doing it. And George. George every day. George talking to her sometimes on the bus or when they met in the corridor; and looking at her with that 'liking' look in his grey eyes . . . Years of school yet, years of all this sort of thing going on happening . . .

The days were drawing in, and Anne jumped off the bus as the rays of the setting sun shone level down the street. She hurried home, opened the door – and found her neighbour's daughter, Nellie, there instead of Gran.

'Where's Gran?'

Nellie looked at her almost accusingly.

'I'm afraid she's had a bit of an accident. She fell down the stairs. I happened to look in – I generally do every day when you're at school – and she'd got herself up, but she was very shaky. We've had the doctor and he says she's to stay in bed today and tomorrow.'

Anne flung her satchel down and darted up the stairs.

'Gran! What've you been doing, Gran?'

She slowed down and walked softly into the room, bending over the bed. Gran didn't look at her, though she turned her head uneasily.

'Is that you, Anne?'

'Yes, Gran. Are you all right?'

'I will be, in a day or two. Silly old thing. I fell down the stairs – it was that corner at the bottom.'

'I shouldn't have left you on your own, Gran,' Anne reproached herself.

'Nonsense. You've got to go to school.'

Anne knelt at the side of the bed. Gran was so small, she hardly made a hump under the bedclothes.

'Shall I put the light on?'

'No, don't bother yet.'

'Shall I bring your tea?'

'Yes, I'd like a cup of tea.'

'Right, I'll just change. Won't be a minute.'

She went down to put the kettle on. Nellie was getting ready to leave.

'I'd better go now. I've to get tea for mother and finish the school off.'

Anne remembered she was the school cleaner and caretaker.

'Thank you,' she said rather awkwardly.

'I'm glad I could help your Gran. What about tomorrow?'

Anne ran her fingers through her hair.

'I don't know yet. We'll let you know when we've talked about it.'

Nellie pulled her cardigan round her chest and went.

Anne made the tea and carried it up carefully.

'Is that you, Anne?'

'Yes, Gran.'

'Put the light on, will you?'

The trouble was – that Anne had switched the light on as she came through the door.

'Why don't you put the light on?'

Anne put the tray down and walked slowly to the bed.

'Gran – can't you see the light's on?'

In the silence they could hear the slow, gentle tick of the clock downstairs.

'No, Anne, I can't see the light. It looks as if I can't see any more . . .'

So what could you do? No use running for the doctor, Gran said he'd told her it might happen like this.

'I'll help you sit up and have your drink of tea, Gran. Perhaps it was the shock. What did the doctor say?'

'He didn't say much that I can remember. To tell the truth I felt that shook up I don't remember much about it. Nellie came in and she went for the doctor – and she's been here most of the time since. She'll have to go, her mother's on her own, and there's the school to see to.'

'She's just gone.'

'And then I seemed to doze until I heard you come in. And I thought it must be late because it had got so dark. But it wasn't that, was it?'

Anne shook her head, uselessly, but she couldn't trust her voice. She put a pillow behind the old, white head with tender care, and then held the cup of tea she'd prepared to Gran's mouth.

'Have a drink, Gran. Make you feel better.'

Ma always had a drink of tea when the going was bad.

A bit dribbled down her chin, and Anne wiped it away with her hankie. Little by little Gran sipped half the cupful and seemed to enjoy it. Then she turned her head away.

'I didn't tell you, Anne, but they said at the hospital this might happen.'

'What about the operation? It's three weeks yet till that.'

'That may make it better.'

MAY? Anne had thought it was for sure. And how were they going to manage the next three weeks? She took a deep gulp of breath and forced her voice to work properly.

'Then we'll just have to wait, won't we, Gran? It won't be long.'

'I'll manage all right while you're at school if you put things out for me.'

'Yes, and go falling down stairs again!'

'No – you could leave me downstairs when you went, and I'd stay there.'

'We'll see, Gran. Don't worry tonight. You've had a nasty fall. I'll stay home tomorrow anyway. We'll see what the doctor and Miss Garfield say.'

Gran dozed most of the evening. The shock of the fall

had left her feeling very frail. Anne moved around as quietly as she could, and when she had done all that needed doing, she sat looking at the fire and stroking Sammy. She hadn't done her homework – she hadn't the heart to, and what was the use? She wouldn't be going to school tomorrow. Goodness knew when she would go again.

And the team? Two weeks to the competition. What would they think? She couldn't tell them the truth. Once it got around that Gran was blind, they'd have her in hospital quick as a knife – and she'd hate that. She'd hate it so much she might even die, little and old as she was. She'd heard Ma talking about old people who went into hospital and 'only came out in a box'.

So she'd got to keep quiet about it, and they wouldn't know why she stayed away. They'd think her a . . . the ugly word that had once been so familiar escaped her for the first time in weeks. It seemed ugly in Gran's kitchen. But she couldn't think of anything that said better what she knew they'd call her.

No more practices. No more splendid feeling of getting better and better and the fun of it all and George and Janet and William and the others . . .

Just little old Gran upstairs. Not able to see the light.

Chapter 14

Hearing the school bus pass the end of the street in the morning was truly horrible.

'My! Anne Moby worryin' because she can't go to school! That's GOT to be the day!' she jeered at herself, trying to remember the days she'd played truant in Leeds, the kid catcher coming round and her hiding till he'd gone away. But it wasn't any use. She minded. Because of that competition.

She did all the things she'd seen Gran do, and then went to the village shop while Nellie-next-door stayed with Gran for half an hour.

'Hello, Anne. Not at school today?' the shop-keeper greeted her.

She hesitated. Should she admit she'd stayed home to look after Gran? Wouldn't they know anyway? Everyone seemed to tell everyone everything here. They wouldn't have missed the doctor's visits. Nellie would have had a story to tell, too. So it wasn't much use saying she'd missed the bus or she'd stayed home because she wasn't well herself. They'd know. But to admit it might get to the authorities.

She compromised by shaking her head and not replying.

The shopping didn't take long, and then she was home again. And it was still only half way through the morning. She had tidied the house and done the vegetables for dinner, and she couldn't see anything else that needed doing. She couldn't go even as far as the garden in case Gran called and she didn't hear her. And yet Gran didn't really seem to want her, she just seemed to want to lie and doze, and not to be bothered by anyone.

She did last night's homework with meticulous care. Just in case . . .

She swept the grate and polished the dresser.

She made a cake. It smelt lovely and she felt rewarded when Gran asked for a piece with her tea.

But the day seemed to crawl by. The big old clock kept ticking, but surely the hands had stopped moving?

It was worse than when she was in Care. That had been a big building and she could wander round it and stretch her legs; and they went out part of every day, to school or somewhere.

How did people – old people – live, keeping in the house like this? Her limbs seemed to jerk and twitch at the inactivity, and she kept walking to the window to see what was happening in the street – only to find nothing was happening.

At last the children from the village school went home. The school bus would be coming soon . . . They would be having the last lesson now . . . now they would be hurrying along to get their coats and race each other to the bus . . . now the bus would be starting, making its way past all the traffic of the other cars and coaches collecting from school . . . now it would be on the way home. George and William would be on the back seat . . . Had Jenny missed her? Would she wonder what had happened?

She longed to go to the gate and see them get off the bus, but felt she must keep out of the way so they wouldn't be able to ask why she'd stayed away. She must make them think she was ill, or that she was just staying off . . . Or they might take Gran away!

Half-past four. They'd be gone now. Nellie was coming back from cleaning the village school. Gran had had tea. Five hours to bed time . . . She prowled to and fro.

She had found the 'nursing' difficult, too. She, who had had so little physical contact with others, had to attend Gran's every need – wash her – everything. And they couldn't ask for the district nurse to come, because then they would have to admit their difficulties. The Doctor didn't seem to think of such things. He had come and said Gran was getting on nicely – but he didn't seem concerned with the everyday problem of how they were going to manage in the meantime, until Gran could have the operation and get cured. He saw his patient was well cared for, and that seemed enough.

Anne took the radio upstairs and listened to it with Gran. An hour passed like that. She fed Sammy. She took Gran a drink of warm milk and a biscuit. She took away one of the pillows and smoothed the sheet.

'Now you be careful with that fire, Anne! Make sure the guard's right in front of it. And I hope you haven't left too big a fire? Move the rug back so nothing can fall on it. Have you fed Sammy? Is he all right? Has he gone out? . . . What about the lamp – don't forget to switch all the lights off! I'd like my candle here, even if I can't see it; I'd like it to be here . . . Have you made firelighters for morning? What are you going to do tomorrow? I reckon you'd best get back to school. You're missin' your lessons. I'll be all right . . . Nellie will look in and give me a bit of dinner . . . You'd best be gettin' off to bed if you're to catch that bus in the morning. I'll try to call you, but . . . I don't seem to wake up the same, now I don't see the light.'

'Nonsense, Gran!' said Anne, forgetting her day-long fretting when she saw how uncomplainingly Gran dealt with her own really bad troubles. 'You go to sleep. And don't get playing with those matches in the night. I'll call you in plenty of time for your breakfast. And Sammy's eaten all his supper and gone out, and the guard's in front of the fire an' everything. And don't worry about me and school. They say I can stay home till you go to hospital.'

What a good thing I learned to tell whoppers! Anne thought, admiring her own performance.

'Oh! That's good of them. That's really good of them. Perhaps Miss Garfield arranged it?'

'Yes, 'spect so,' lied Anne glibly. 'Now you go to sleep. It's past your bedtime.'

She left the bedroom doors open so she could hear Gran in the night. And although she didn't feel a bit tired she went to bed and tried to lie still. But she couldn't sleep. She puzzled over the competition, counting the days to and fro, till Gran went into hospital, and till the competition. It was no use. Apart from missing the necessary everyday practice, the competition was at least a week before the operation.

Could she ask Miss Garfield? What could Miss Garfield do? Pay for someone to come and mind Gran? It would cost too much. And who? And why should she?

Nellie? Gran wouldn't be safe with Nellie's sporadic visits, and Nellie had too much to do already with her job and her mother ill. No, she must stay home and manage herself. If it hadn't been for Gran and Miss Garfield she'd not be here to be in any competition. She'd be in that Borstal. In Leeds. Or worse . . . So what was she mithering about?

If Ma suddenly appeared, and Ma really was Gran's daughter, and Ma looked after Gran – it was a lovely dream for a while, but she couldn't keep up her confidence in it. Ma was long gone. Ma come back? Why should she? And if she did, she'd never been one for looking after people. And deep down Anne felt that Ma was one thing and Gran another. Somehow she could not truly believe Ma was Gran's Mary.

The church clock struck eleven. She twisted on her other side, hoping Gran was so soundly asleep she wouldn't hear her. Competition! Competition! was echoing inside her head. Gran gave an unhappy little moan and Anne leapt out of bed to go to her.

'What time is it?'

'It's eleven o'clock. Anything you want?'

'I'd like a sip of water, Anne.'

Anne lifted the frail old head with its silky, thin hair, with a care she hadn't known she possessed.

'Thank you. You're not asleep yet?'

'I was, Gran. I just woke up.'

'Well, you go back to bed. You'll catch cold. I'll be all right now.'

Anne smoothed the sheet again and went back to her own room. No use thinking about her problems. She'd be awake all night. Her thoughts drifted to the Mowbrays instead.

She saw the mossy cross; and the glint of water in the deep well. She began to think about it as it might have been, when the well was in the castle courtyard. Flagged. With buildings all round with arches, like the church door arch. And horses, lovely horses like the one in the park. Three horses. One for the groom. Was that what you called him? One for her. That one was white, with a blue cloth under the saddle and the harness soft and shining light brown. And one black horse. And someone came out from under the arches and leapt on its back like George leapt over the vaulting horse . . . and they wheeled round and rode out of the courtyard into the sunshine. Somewhere the day-dream turned into a sleep-dream. The boy who rode with her was older now. Mowbray looked as it did today, with crowding tree-trunks ... He came from between them wearing the deer-skin tunic she usually thought of him wearing.

He looked serious ...

'You're the last of the Mowbrays,' he said.

She turned to answer and found she was awake and daylight was showing through the curtains.

That day was much the same as the one before, except that in the end, just as the light was beginning to go, Mrs Clarke came visiting.

'I've come to sit with your Gran for a bit,' she said. 'I expect she'd like a bit of a gossip. I hear she's having trouble with her eyes.'

'Yes,' said Anne.

'Wouldn't you like to get out a bit while I'm here? I'll stay till the clock strikes seven.'

It was no use worrying about the rumours that would go round when Mrs Clarke had talked to Gran. After all, Nellie came every day. She might as well make the most of her chance to get out. She pulled her anorak on as she went and hurried into Mowbray. Once there, she ran helter-skelter, as fast as she could, until she was at the foot of the cross in the very middle of the wood. At that she was hardly out of breath; she was so fit after all the exercises for the competition.

She stood on the steps of the cross in the low rays of the setting sun. Then she leapt down. She glanced around and saw no one was in sight. It was no use, of course, because she was never going to get back to school in time; but out of a kind of nostalgia for the good times, she started on some of the dance for the competition. There was no music except what was in her head, but she hummed to herself. She was so wrapped in her dance that she did not notice she was no longer alone. William and George were standing at the edge of the trees. She stopped abruptly.

'You missed practice yesterday and today,' William said accusingly.

She had nothing to say.

'Why aren't you at school? You don't look ill!'

It was no use trying to plead illness when they'd seen her dancing like that. She knew she looked anything but ill. Certainly not ill enough to stay away from practice.

'When are you coming back?'

'Not for more than two weeks.'

'Why?'

'Can't tell you.'

'Well, you ought to be in school anyway. It's against the law to stay away for nothing,' William said piously.

'We'll have to put someone in your place if you're not back tomorrow,' said George.

'I won't be back.'

'They won't be as good, and we'll probably lose.'

'Well, I can't help it.'

'Why can't you help it? I think you're doing it a-purpose.'

'No, I'm not!'

'They say your Gran's ill,' said George.

Anne nodded.

'Well, you can't stay away every time she's ill. Especially with the competition. Other people manage.'

'I think you just don't care. I think you're doing it a-purpose,' William repeated. 'You don't DESERVE to be in the team.'

Distantly the church clock began to strike.

It was no use trying to explain. Anne turned and ran away along the path.

'Spoil sport! You don't care! Rotten thing you are!'

The words pursued her, fast as she ran.

Mrs Clarke was waiting at the gate.

'She seems well enough in herself,' she said. 'It's a pity about her eyes, but I expect she'll be better after the operation. It's a good thing you can stay and look after her.'

And the good lady hurried home to her own family.

'A good thing!' Anne muttered bitterly, pausing to shake the tears from her eyes and get her voice steady before she went inside.

And then later, when it was dark, a chant started up in the road.

'Spoil sport! Spoil sport! Anny Moby, spoil sport . . .'

She hurried outside, but whoever it was had vanished when they heard the door open. As soon as she was back in the house the chant started again.

'Anne Moby, spoil sport. Don't care was made to care. Don't care was hung . . . Spoil sport. Afraid to leave Granny and go to school. Anne Moby, spoil sport . . .'

She rushed outside and shouted into the empty street. 'You lot go away! You're waking my Gran!'

'Granny's darling!' came back from the shadows lower down the road. 'You're waking my Gran! Boo-hoo. Pity you came here, Anne Moby. Go back to Leeds.'

'That's enough!' a voice protested. But whoever it was was shouted down.

It was Nellie coming out from next door and telling them what she'd do if they didn't clear off and go home that sent them away in the end. Anne went back into the house and closed the door.

'Who was that?' Gran called.

'Some of the kids shouting about,' Anne said airily, glad

for once that Gran couldn't see her face.

'I thought I heard your name.'

'It was only a joke. They've gone now.'

When the jobs were all done and the house was quiet at last Anne could think over what had happened. She'd show them! She wouldn't be in their damned competition not if they asked her. They could get stuffed. She'd done her best and at the first sign of trouble they turned on her. Because she didn't belong. She wasn't one of the village ones. So they came and disgraced her like that. Let them wait! When Gran was better and she was free again, she'd show the lot of them.

She lay in the dark biting her lower lip. Because it was all right thinking that way, but how miserable to be with them all when they weren't friends any more; when they wouldn't talk to her or play with her. When George looked like that and William shouted at her.

And Ma wasn't going to come back. And Gran was BLIND.

But she wouldn't allow herself to cry.

Just because I'm a girl, that's no excuse, she thought scornfully. Anyway, I'm a MOWBRAY. He said I was!

So she lay stiff and still in bed disregarding the heavy tears that found their way down her cheeks.

Chapter 15

The next day the doctor said Gran could get up, but she mustn't try to walk downstairs, and he would arrange for John Duffield from the inn at the corner to drop by at eleven o'clock to carry her down and again at six o'clock to carry her back. That made it a better day. There was the busy-ness of arranging what Gran should wear that would be warm and easy to put on; and of getting everything ready for her arrival downstairs; and then John Duffield coming and he stayed for a drink of tea and a piece of the cake Anne had made and he complimented her on it. And Gran's pleasure at being downstairs in her own chair again. She seemed to feel it was lighter and brighter down there, even if she couldn't see. And Sammy was pleased. He'd investigated upstairs to see where Gran had got to, but it wasn't his proper place and he had retreated. Now he stretched on the mat feeling that his world was more-or-less to rights again.

It left Anne a bit more free, too. Gran could be left alone while she went to the shop and she could go and stand in the sunshine and pick a few fresh flowers from the garden, knowing Gran was within call through the open door. If it hadn't been for those echoes in the dark – 'Anne Moby, spoil sport . . .' she wouldn't have minded so much. Except that today was Thursday. Tomorrow would be Friday – just one week before the competition. Who would they put in her place? There was the Reserve, Christine, but she wasn't really good . . . Anne realised how the others felt at having the even standard of their team spoiled. But . . .

She heard the bus arrive, even though she was indoors. She wished she could just explain, so they didn't hate her so . . . if she could just run up and talk for a minute to them she wouldn't mind the rest so much . . . Silly! She knew it was impossible. Better get tea ready instead.

Just then there was a knock at the door, and she could hardly believe her eyes when she saw George and William and a girl she didn't know, apart from seeing her on the bus, standing there.

'Who is it, Anne?' Gran called.

'Some kids from school.'

'Can you come out and talk?' George asked awkwardly, while the girl looked at Anne appraisingly.

'Just going out a minute, Gran,' Anne called. 'You'll be all right? You won't move about? I'll get tea ready as soon as I'm back.'

'I'll just sit here,' Gran promised.

Anne went up the path and the others followed her to the gate.

'It's about the competition,' George explained. 'We tried Christine today but it doesn't work. We heard you had to stay home because your Gran's gone blind. That right?'

Anne nodded.

'Why didn't you say?' demanded William.

'If the school knew they might say she couldn't look after me properly and I'd have to go back to Leeds. Or they might put her in a home. She'll be all right when she's had her operation – I think. Just got to wait till then.'

'We want you back for the competition. This is Brenda. She's my sister. And she says she'll look after your Gran tomorrow, and then you could come to the practice. And one of the others would come every day next week.'

Anne's heart leapt with delight at the reprieve; but then she was less sure.

'Would Gran be all right?'

' 'Course she would. Our Brenda looked after Mam when she was ill last year – and all the rest of us too.'

'What would school say? And your Mam?'

'They'd not know. Brenda'll come here instead of getting on the bus, that's all. And then Lily Atkinson says she'll do Monday, and Brenda could do Tuesday again – it's only six days.'

'I'd have to ask Gran.'

'Yes. See what she says.'

How could she explain something so complicated? And after she'd let Gran think it was all right for her to stay off school.

The others followed her back down the path.

'Gran – do you know Brenda Moore?'

' 'Course I do. Her Granny and me went to school together. Knew her father when he was a boy, too.'

'They've come to see if I could go to school tomorrow to practise for that competition I told you about – if Brenda came to mind you for me. What d'you think?'

'That's all right,' Gran said placidly. 'I didn't like you being off school all that time anyway. I'll be all right with Brenda. But what about her going to school?'

'It doesn't matter missing one day. And she's not in the competition. And Lily Atkinson would come on Monday, and then Brenda would do another day. Sure that's OK?'

She couldn't keep the eagerness out of her voice, and Gran heard it plainly enough.

'Is Brenda there? Tell her it's very good of her and that's quite all right.'

Brenda and George were listening at the door. They

127

nodded to show they understood.

'See you at the bus tomorrow,' George said.

'Mmn. If Brenda is here before I go.'

And they left.

It was so good, Anne felt a bit guilty. How could she feel so happy about a grotty old competition when Gran was in such trouble? And was it safe to leave her with Brenda? And Lily Atkinson?

Gran seemed to know what was in her mind.

She's amazing! thought Anne, seeing how she managed to drink her tea by herself now – she'd learned so quickly and she managed so well. And she seemed to understand everything going on around her.

'Don't you go worrying about leaving me,' said Gran. 'I could manage for myself really if John carried me down and Nellie looked in – but if young Brenda's here in case I want anything, and to help me move around a bit – I get so stiff sitting all the time – we'll manage quite all right. You get back to school and your lessons and that competition. I don't want you turning out a dunce like your Ma was . . .'

It was the first time she had ever suggested that she really believed her daughter was Anne's mother.

'Yes, Gran. And I'll do ever so well. There's only eight of us picked from the whole first year.'

'Um,' said Gran, not wanting her to get a swelled head by too much approval.

Anne practised all the exercises and steps, barefooted, in the kitchen after John Duffield had carried Gran upstairs. She put everything ready for morning. Gran seemed to catch her happiness and settled down contentedly for the night. She hated to be a responsibility and a nuisance. Now she could get downstairs again, and Anne could be in her competition – that Brenda wouldn't mind a day off if she was anything like her father! – Gran felt more independent again. She tried to count the days to her operation. That would mean hospital, but she wouldn't mind it for a few days. It was going into a place like that to live, away from all her things, away from where she had lived with Albert, that she had dreaded. Perhaps it would all come right. That child seemed to bring luck with her, she really did. She hoped they won that competition . . .

Anne woke early and had given Gran her breakfast and seen her washed and comfortable by bus time. And Brenda appeared in good time, took off her coat, and seemed to know just what to do.

'Gran's to stay where she is till John Duffield comes to carry her down,' Anne explained.

Brenda looked at her curiously, surprised that this girl she didn't really know should be so stupid as to suppose that she, Brenda, fourteen years old, couldn't manage a house and an old woman for a day when she'd managed the farm and all the family before now. But she was a placid girl, and accepted people and circumstances as they came, so she put it down to being brought up in Leeds, nodded her understanding, and left it at that.

Anne ran up the road, anxious to be quite sure of catching the bus.

The formalities of explaining her absence, of dealing with the out-of-date homework she handed in and the new work the others had started, were unimportant and sorted out without much trouble. The day's climax was the lunch hour practice. Would she have forgotten? The others looked a bit dubious. Several of them still resented her staying away, although the word had gone round that it wasn't her fault. Those with more secure families found it hard to believe family trouble could get in the way of things so important to themselves. Two or three, themselves from broken homes, understood though. As did George.

It wasn't brilliant, but it was all right. They had time to run through the programme twice, and the second time it was almost as good as it used to be.

'Monday ought to see it OK,' said the team leader. 'Will you be here, Anne?'

'Yes,' said Anne, crossing her fingers behind her back.

Then it was a matter of waiting impatiently for the afternoon to end; for the others to get on the bus; for the bus to get to Kirkeby; for her to run down the road and into the house and make sure everything was all right.

Brenda had been sitting on the settee, but she got to her feet and began to put her coat on.

'You all right, Gran?'

'Hello, Anne! Yes. Brenda and I've got on well, haven't we?'

'Yes,' said Brenda, with her slow smile.

'She's started some knitting for me, and I can manage a bit.'

Anne hadn't thought of that. She hadn't been taught to knit and sew until she came to the village, and she wasn't good at either.

'Thanks!' she said, turning to Brenda admiringly.

Brenda quietly made her way to the door.

'Good afternoon, Mrs Moby.'

'Good afternoon, Brenda. Thank your mother for me, won't you?'

Brenda didn't explain that her mother didn't know about this arrangement; but she felt sure she would have approved if she had known. All the village thought well of Mrs Moby and would try to help her.

Anne ran upstairs and changed her clothes, and chattered like a load of monkeys while she prepared tea. School had seemed so exciting after missing it all those days. And the practice!

She stayed home all evening. Nellie came in and sorted the knitting out, which Anne hadn't been able to do. Mrs Clarke came in as she was passing. And Anne didn't need to do anything exciting, she was content just to be there, her head full of next week's events.

That night no unkind voices called down the street. Gran and Anne slept peacefully.

On Monday Lily's day didn't go so smoothly. She was a bit late coming and Anne, who wouldn't leave till she was there, almost missed the bus. And when she came home in the evening, Gran was a bit ruffled and bothered and Lily was waiting impatiently to go. Anne wondered what would happen in two days' time – they'd not arranged anything yet; and Lily's turn clearly hadn't worked out as well as Brenda's.

Next morning she found the problem was even more immediate. Brenda said she had exams at school the rest of the week and she and George had been talking and they agreed she mustn't miss them. They all met at break, and Anne wasn't surprised when Lily Atkinson refused to take another turn. She didn't like school, but she'd disliked her solitary day even less, let alone old Mrs Moby's unspoken criticism of the way she'd done things, which she'd felt clearly enough.

'My mam says I mustn't do it any more. I ought to be at school,' she said virtuously.

The others suspected Mam knew nothing about it, but there was no point in arguing.

It happened that most of those who had left the village

school that year were boys; and they didn't like to spread the tale too wide among other classes, apart from George's sister which was different. The shrill bell rang for them to go inside before anything was decided. As soon as morning school was over it was practice time; and then they had to hurry for the last sitting of lunch. They couldn't talk openly over the meal because of the strangers among them.

'I'll just have to stay home tomorrow, anyway,' said Anne, as the remorseless bell rang again and they had to start afternoon school.

There was no chance to talk again until they were getting on the bus to go home. Anne took her usual seat near the front, but as he passed George tipped his head back in the familiar 'Come here!' sign. Puzzled, she followed him and William to the back seat and stood waiting. She knew she could not be expected to sit on the back seat that was their special place. So she stood, bending forward to hear what they said, as the bus started jerkily.

'D'you think William could manage your Gran tomorrow?' George asked.

For a moment Anne was speechless. Would it be 'sissy' looking after an old lady all day and getting her dinner for her? And what about when she wanted to go to the bathroom?

Anne looked at William. He wasn't flashy like George all fair hair and blue eyes and best-at-everything. He wasn't in the competition. But it took guts to offer to do a thing like that, when it was bound to get out that he had.

She thought quickly. She could leave everything ready; and Gran was so sensible she could tell him how to set about things. And William was sensible too, he must know simple things like making a drink of tea and how to help an old lady out of her chair and safely back again . . .

But would Gran like it?

'Can we ask Gran? I think it'd be all right. And THANKS!'

She retreated to her own seat, her mind confused. That she, Anne Moby, who she suspected didn't really belong in the village, as they'd said, should be so important that really important people like George and William should scheme to give her help because they *needed* her . . .

But what about the next two days – Thursday, and the famous Friday when the competition happened? Surely something would turn up! If tomorrow had been sorted out in such an unlooked for way, something was bound to turn up.

George and William went home with her. Gran and Brenda looked so busy and contented it seemed almost a pity to disturb them.

'Gran,' said Anne, 'I've brought Brenda's brother, George, and William Metcalfe home. Brenda can't come again because of her exams.'

'Yes, she told me,' said Mrs Moby. 'But don't you worry, I'm getting really clever, aren't I, Brenda? I'll be able to manage for a couple of days.'

To show how clever she was she got to her feet, forgetting Brenda had put a cup of tea on the table beside her, and her arm caught the cup and swept it to the floor. It fell on the rug, so the cup didn't break, but the hot tea caught her skirt and she felt it. Anne darted forward with a cloth to mop it up.

'Now don't you get being so clever, our Gran,' she said firmly. 'Just because you're as nimble as can be doesn't mean you can do as you like all the time! She does marvels, doesn't she, Brenda? And she can do lots of things better than I can, now. But then she starts to show off . . .' and she chattered away until Gran was tidy and seated again and her embarrassment at her mistake was forgotten.

'You see, Gran,' Anne went on, 'you manage so well, we wondered if you'd mind having a boy instead, tomorrow, because Brenda can't come.'

'A boy? Who'd that be?'

'William Metcalfe. He's here now.'

'Oh yes. I remember him being born. And his mother was a friend of our Mary once. Does he want to come? Surely not!'

William cleared his throat.

'I'd like to, Mrs Moby,' he said. 'I don't know how good I'd be.'

'Well – if you're sure . . . it's very good of you.'

'No trouble.'

'I'm sure we'd manage fine.'

'You can teach him to cook, Gran. And he could chop some wood for us and sort out the coalshed, couldn't he?'

And so it was arranged.

And when Anne got home the next afternoon, hurrying because she wasn't really sure how William would manage, she found he was playing cat's cradle with Gran, and everything as neat and comfy as you please. Anne could have hugged him.

'Thank you!' she said, shining-eyed.

'Wasn't nothing. How'd practice go?' William asked.

'Smashing. We've got the best music, too, and it all fits together – better than the others'.'

'What about tomorrow?'

Anne turned to Gran.

'Would you mind if I had someone to stay with me for two nights? She could sleep with me.'

'Who is it?'

'Jenny – you know, Jenny-from-Newlands. Her

mother's not well, and they're going to Newlands again. Tonight. And Jenny thinks her mother won't mind if you don't. So they're going to call on their way through. And she could stay till Friday night.'

'Good idea,' said William.

'I don't mind,' said Mrs Moby. 'What a pity about her mother! She always was a nervous one . . .'

William left, and walking with him to the gate, Anne felt that if she lived to be even older than Gran she'd never forget how good he'd been. And then she set to work on her jobs and her homework and hearing about Gran's day and helping sort out Gran's knitting, so that really she was learning to knit quite decently herself, and Gran felt she was being clever to teach her even if she couldn't see . . .

And all the time Anne was listening for a car to stop. Suppose Jenny's granddad said she wasn't to stay? Suppose they didn't come? She'd not have Jenny then – her very first friend-to-stay ever. And she'd not be able to go to school tomorrow for the last rehearsal . . .

But the car did stop. They all came in and the little cottage was pleasantly crowded, and Gran was quite flushed with pleasure, because apart from her present troubles, people had got out of the habit of visiting since Albert was gone. Now there was conversation, and Anne made a drink of tea; and it was nice to hear old Mr Wright again – such a wise old chap as he always was! And Winnie, poor thing . . . But she'd be better for some peace and quiet up at Newlands.

It was almost a party.

When they had gone it seemed very quiet, with the clock ticking and Sammy asking for his supper, and only the sweet and gentle voice of this Jenny, mingling with the hardly suppressed excitement of Anne's.

Bless them all!

For the first time ever Anne shared her bed. They couldn't talk much because of disturbing Gran, but they whispered until they were hoarse, and until Jenny found she was slipping asleep between sentences. Anne, touch-me-not Anne, lay awake longer, feeling rather than hearing Jenny's soft breathing.

I may be the last of the Mowbrays, she thought, drifting into her favourite falling-asleep dream. But Jenny's got something older even that that.

She remembered the day of the buttercup-and-daisy chains, and the flowers floating down the stream when they had to go back to school. They had crowned Jenny then – queen – queen of the summer. That's what she was!

Chapter 16

The competition was in a way a bit of a let-down after all. The school as a whole wasn't very interested in it, apart from the rivalry of trying to win for their own year. Not a lot of them liked gymnastics and that sort of dance, to do, let alone watch. And the older they got the more this seemed so. The first year, being youngest, had the best chance from the start, with their fresh enthusiasm. And they were not so bedevilled with exams. By Friday it was generally thought that Year 1 would win. And they did.

It was twenty minutes of colourful excitement and effort; and then rather boring watching all the others. There was the brief glory of going up for the cup, while everyone clapped and cheered as if it was the FA Cup. And then it was all over.

Anne felt a great sense of relaxation, going home in the bus, as the familiar hedges slid by. It was safely over; she hadn't let them down, in fact it seemed to have made her one of them as never before – the boys too. And now she could stay at home as long as Gran needed her, with no more need for contrivance. And when – she wouldn't say *if* even to herself – Gran was better, she would get on with this business of school.

Jenny was waiting at the bus stop – unlike when she was at the village school, this one would take her almost home. And so back to Gran. Peacefully.

A letter from Miss Garfield was delivered while Anne was having breakfast next morning. Gran still had hers in bed, and Anne had seen to that – and now she was waiting for John Duffield to come and carry her down.

'Wonder what this is about?' mused Anne, reading the letter. 'If she wants to come and see me she's going to find out Gran can't see . . .'

The letter was startling.

'I am coming on Saturday morning to bring you to Leeds. I am afraid this is very short notice, but something has come up that must be attended to then. I hope you can be ready by 10.30 when I arrive. If you feel you cannot leave Mrs Moby, she could come with us. I will explain in more detail when I see you.

Sincerely,
Julia Garfield'

What could it mean?

She couldn't go to Leeds for the day! After all that contriving, just when she thought there were no more problems – to have to contrive for another day. Gran wouldn't understand if she was rushed off to Leeds like that. And what could it all be about? It must be about her living with Gran. It could only mean trouble.

Or was it about Ma? After all this time Anne felt something like terror at the idea of Ma hurt – or dead. Those car accidents. You heard about them all the time.

She pushed her breakfast aside, unable to face the food on her plate.

'Are there any letters, Anne? I thought I heard the postman,' Gran called.

'Letter from Miss Garfield. She's coming this morning.'

'Oh dear! Is the house nice and tidy? I'd better get up.'

'No, you stay where you are till John Duffield comes. I'll come and help you dress in a minute.'

Gran was right, it was important to get the place straight so Miss Garfield could see that they managed all right. No time to worry about Ma and the Leeds business till that was done.

Miss Garfield was early arriving in the village, and although the breakfast dishes were tidied away and the hearth swept, Gran was still upstairs. Anne had to explain.

'How has she been managing while you were at school?'

Anne told her about staying away, and how her friends had helped her, and about the competition and how they'd won. Perhaps it would please Miss Garfield and stop her minding about them missing school.

Just then John came and carried Gran down and installed her in her chair.

'I haven't told her about going to Leeds,' Anne said under her breath. 'I can't leave her alone, you see.'

Miss Garfield thought it looked worse and worse. Any authority that knew this child was in the charge of a blind old lady of over seventy who was being given money to keep her – a child playing truant from school and her friends doing the same to mind 'Gran' . . . What a scandal! It would make the headlines. And yet she felt it was really quite splendid that they'd managed so well, and all shared and helped.

'Come and see our garden, Miss Garfield,' said Anne, in what she realised was an artificial voice and an unnatural way. But she had to get her outside somehow.

'What's this about?' she asked urgently, as soon as they were safely out of hearing distance. 'Is it Ma?'

'Yes, Anne. She's come back.'

'Is she all right?'

'Yes. She's very well. She's got a job working in a

hospital. She's on her own now. The man you called 'Dad' has left her.'

'He wasn't my Dad.'

'No. Your father was a student who went exploring in the Hindu Kush – in Asia – and I'm afraid he was killed. He was lost and he's never been heard of since.'

'What was his name?'

'Robert Moby.'

'So he might have been a Mowbray . . . Not Ma. I didn't think she was. And she's all right?'

'She's fine. And she wants you back. We're to meet her in John Lambert's office at twelve o'clock.'

'I can't leave Gran.'

'You must. If we don't meet your mother she'll make a great fuss and you'll certainly be taken away from Gran, and we'd all get in trouble, probably – including Gran.'

'But I can't leave Gran alone, and there's no one to stay with her!'

'Then we'll have to take her with us. It will be an outing for her.'

How wretched! Anne thought. Bumped about in a motor car when you couldn't see out of the windows or know what was happening. But what else could they do?

'You mustn't tell her!' Anne said fiercely. 'She's got this operation coming and she hasn't got to be worried! She can think I've got to go to Leeds about the allowance or something, but you mustn't tell her about Ma. And Ma can't be her daughter, can she, if she married a Moby? You mustn't tell her that either! She's coming to think I am her grandchild and that her daughter may still be alive somewhere. She's got worries enough without our telling her not.'

Miss Garfield raised her eyebrows at this hectoring, and Anne blushed; but she gazed straight back all the same,

140

her dark level brows emphasising her fierce look.

'Well – I have to take care of Gran, see, and there isn't time to wrap it up.'

Miss Garfield laid a restraining hand on her arm as they turned back to the house.

'I understand,' she said quietly. 'But there's something you must understand too. If your mother wants you back, I can't stop her taking you. Nor can John Lambert nor anyone else.'

'I can!' said Anne. 'I won't go. Not now. Not till Gran's better.'

'Anne, you MUST understand. You would HAVE to go.'

Anne's black brows were still almost drawn together in a fierce, straight line. She turned to go indoors without another word.

Miss Garfield knew what the law said. Could Anne fight that?

It was eleven o'clock already. In another hour they would know.

Chapter 17

Gran was rather flurried at the suggestion of a trip to Leeds, but Anne pointed out what a nice morning it was for a 'ride-out', and that she would only have to sit in the car or in Miss Garfield's house, not walk about or have to meet strangers . . . Gran could hear the worry in her voice. She didn't know what this sudden 'business' was all about; but Anne had been very good to her since her accident, and if she could help now by not making a fuss, she would. So she had her hat put on, and her coat, and was given her handbag and assured by Anne that she looked 'a treat'; and that Sammy had been fed and the fire had a guard in front and would be safe. At the end of all that Anne turned to run upstairs to get herself ready, but Miss Garfield, looking more and more anxiously at her watch, said there wasn't time. Anne's jeans were clean and neat enough, and she was wearing a clean shirt. She picked up a comb and ran it through her hair as they got into the car.

Gran found the little car surprisingly comfortable; and despite her feeling of urgency, Miss Garfield drove quietly and steadily. She chatted about where they were and what she could see; and when they got to the outskirts of Leeds where the noise of the traffic might have been worrying, she turned the car radio on so Gran could listen to the familiar programmes. Before Anne really had time to sort out her feelings and thoughts they had arrived at the car park outside John Lambert's office.

'I'll take Gran to my house to wait,' explained Miss Garfield. 'John Lambert's office is through that door, straight up the stairs and the first room on the right. He'll phone me when you've finished, and I'll come and pick you up.'

She got out of the car and let Anne out from the back. She stood watching her as she walked, very straight-backed, to the big entrance door. The clock in the tower struck twelve.

Anne did not glance back. She went on, ran up the stairs, heard a voice call for her to 'Come in!', opened the door, and took in the scene before her.

John Lambert sat with his back to the light, behind a desk littered with papers and wire trays. To his right, and rather in the shadow, stood the familiar figure of her mother. She'd forgotten how well she knew her appearance until she saw her again.

Mrs Moby had planned an emotional reunion that would have strengthened her claim. She would open her arms and Anne would run crying to her ... and that would show that snooty Mr Lambert where he got off!

But instead there was this quiet, self-possessed girl, very like Anne but taller, and not quite so skinny, and clean and tidy even if she was in jeans. With good shoes on and her hair looking nice.

'Hello, Ma,' said Anne. 'You all right?'

'Yes,' her mother answered. 'I'm all right now. I've got a new flat and I'm come to take you home.'

Anne shook her head.

'Can't do that, Ma. I'm wanted where I am.'

'And where's that?'

'I'm with an old woman who thinks I'm her grand-daughter. She's been ever so good to me. And she's had an accident and she can't see, and she's to have an operation on 18 November. I can't go nowhere till she's better.'

She was standing just inside the door, and her mother was standing by the desk, facing her.

'Come and sit down, Anne, and we'll talk about it,' said John Lambert. Like Miss Garfield he was startled to hear of Gran's accident, and that she was blind now.

Anne went forward and sat down. She took a quick look at her mother. She recognised the same best coat – the one she'd missed from the wardrobe when she first realised Ma had left. Memory of that hungry, frightening time, strengthened her resolve.

'You're my girl and you're coming back with me!' Ma blustered. 'Leaving you with a blind old woman! And Granny my aunt – you ain't got a granny as I knows of. And only jeans to wear when you come out. Neglected, that's what you've bin. I'll see you hear more of this,' she went on, turning to Mr Lambert.

'What d'you want me for?' Anne asked curiously. 'You went off and left me before.'

'Well of course I want you. You're my girl aren't you? All those years slogging and slaving . . . I had to leave you then, but you didn't have to go off so I couldn't find yer. Taken me all this time it has. Now, where are your things? You tell me and we'll go and get them, and you'll come home with me.'

Hearing the rising menace in the voice, Anne remembered the strength of Ma's hand when it was raised against her, and almost flinched. But Mr Lambert wouldn't let anyone hit her, not here. All the same she got to her feet and stood behind her chair.

'I'm happy where I am, Ma. And like I say, I'm needed. I might come home some day but I can't come now.'

She looked her mother in the eye, her own dark brows

drawn together; and Mrs Moby was suddenly reminded of that young man, all those years ago, who'd been so wild for her at one time; and then after they'd married he'd had his own way in what he thought was important and gone off . . . But this was only a bit of a kid, her Anne. What would her friends and neighbours say if she let herself be done out of her daughter like this?

'She's got to come with me. That's the law, ain't it?' she demanded of Mr Lambert.

He hesitated.

'I'm afraid it is, Mrs Moby. But Anne really is happy and settled where she is; and your way of life is not so settled or suitable, as you know.'

'I know no such thing! Respectable as anybody I am. Got my own place, got a job. I want my daughter back, and I'm having her, see.'

She advanced to take hold of Anne's arm. But Anne stepped back.

'Don't think I'd make a fuss if I was you, Ma,' she said. 'If it all came out you'd left me alone when you went off, you might find yourself in trouble.'

'That I won't!' blustered her mother. 'I've told them how it was and they've nothin' to say.'

'Have you told them how you and that man you told me to call 'Dad' used to hit me?'

'Hit you? We never did! Little liar you're gettin' to be.'

'Yes you did, and they can tell so from that school I was at, they saw the marks! And they know I'd nothing to wear or anything. Neglected they'll call it.'

Mrs Moby was taken aback for a moment, and looked at Anne shrewdly. She knew her so well that she was able to detect the least bit of hesitation behind her bold statement. Then Mrs Moby remembered that Anne could be led sometimes when she couldn't be driven.

'Come on, Anne,' she wheedled. 'You don't want to spend your life with strangers! You belong with me. And they say they've took you off somewhere in the country. You! What about going to the pictures Saturday nights? And the fish-and-chips after? And the discos at the Club? You don't belong in no country with all that mud and cows and things.'

Anne caught her mother's smile and found herself smiling. Ma had always been able to charm the birds off the trees whatever her faults. She loved to live, to eat and drink and sleep and be warm and have fun. Anne was tempted. Fun. That's what it would be. Staying off school again to have fun. Fun on the streets with all the others. Kirkeby seemed like a picture in a Sunday school book, pretty and insipid. After all this was her MOTHER . . .

But Mrs Moby spoiled it. She wasn't to know.

'You don't want to spend your time with some silly old woman – and blind, too, they say! Bet she's nasty, dirty, too, that age and blind. There's places for such as she. She'll be OK there. You come along with me.'

Anne took a step backward.

'She's not nasty an' dirty, she's sweet – and kind – and brave!' she said, tears springing to her eyes. 'And I won't leave her as long as she wants me. If anything happens to her it might be different. But she's got this operation soon and I'm not leaving her till she's better.'

'You'll have to – won't she?'

'I won't! If you try to make me I'll just run away. And I'll tell everyone how you left me before, and how you carry on with all those men and – everything!'

'You talk to me like that? You keep a polite tongue in your head my girl or you'll be sorry. If that's how they've taught you to talk to your mother, the sooner you're back with me the better.'

John Lambert got to his feet. He saw Anne was not helping her case by the slanging match that was developing. Soon there would be a scene, with her mother dragging her forcibly away, and little he could do about it.

But Anne seemed to realise that herself. She never knew where the idea came from, because it wasn't like her – her way was to fly at Ma tooth and nail, to kick and sctatch if she was held; to shout and swear and hit in a blind temper. She was in a wild temper now. But all of a sudden something came to her, as if it were from outside her head, almost as if she heard words spoken.

'You don't win like that . . .'

The light from the window was dazzling her eyes. Perhaps that distracted her. Certainly instead of the dingy office she seemed conscious of Mowbray and the low light through the trees, and that figure she had never seen – the one she dreamt said, 'The last of the Mowbrays . . .'

For a moment she stood quite still, fighting hard to be cool and sensible – as she MUST be if she and Gran were going to win. Her mother had never known this to happen before. She had braced herself for a physical onslaught – and was like a ship whose sails suddenly lost the wind when Anne became quiet and calm instead. Anne even sat down again, holding hard to the seat of her chair at each side, partly to steel her nerve, partly because they couldn't suddenly snatch her away unless they took the chair too, if she held on.

'Ma, have you told Mr Lambert that you've been drawing Child Allowance for me all this time?'

'What? How'd you know that?' her mother demanded, unwisely, and before she had time to realise what she was admitting.

'I reckon you could go to prison for that. And be made to pay it all back.'

Mrs Moby was flabbergasted. She disliked the prospect of both things. She loved pretty possessions – those shoes she was wearing with nice high heels and a bit of suede on the toes, for instance, she'd bought with that money. Might as well have it till she found out what had happened to Anne, she'd decided . . .

Mr Lambert was suddenly alert. Anne pushed her advantage.

'Now look here, Ma,' she said. 'You know you don't much want me back, not for good. Your blokes don't like it, and now I'm older you can't have them in the flat like you used to. And I'm getting right good at school and I'm going to stay there and get a proper job in the end. So I wouldn't be any use to you. If you carry on this way I'll tell them how you treated me, and Mr Lambert will get you for cheating on the Allowance. Let's make a deal.'

Mrs Moby felt rather helpless.

'Gran is ever so old. I may not be able to live with her all the time till I leave school. If anything happens to Gran I'll come home if you still want me. We can keep in touch through Mr Lambert; he'll always know where I am. And if we can agree about that I expect Mr Lambert'll be able to arrange something about the Allowance; because they don't want a fuss about all this,' she said shrewdly. 'But you'll have to hand over the book and no more funny business.'

Anne knew what she meant, and so did Mr Lambert, but Mrs Moby found it confusing and alarming. She took refuge in pathos.

'Didn't think you'd be so heartless, our Anne,' she said, reaching in her handbag for a tissue.

'Come off it, Ma! You know you'll manage fine, like you always have. And Mr Lambert will let me know if you really need me. Bet you get a new boy friend before the end of next week, in that outfit. New, isn't it, 'cept the coat?'

'You like it?' her mother asked more cheerfully.

' 'Smashin'!'

They smiled at each other, suddenly more alike. The same slightly derisive, slightly damn-all-the-world smile curled both their mouths and glinted in their eyes.

Anne's mother understood. She'd lost, for now at least. So she might as well take it in good part. She looked at Mr Lambert questioningly.

'I think Anne has it about right, Mrs Moby,' he said. 'I understand that you continued to use the Allowance book in error. If you hand it to me now, I'll try to straighten the matter out. And I have your address – Anne could write to you regularly. As she says, circumstances may change in the future.'

Anne shook her head.

'Ma's not one for writing letters,' she explained. 'But I could meet her in Leeds sometimes, p'raps?'

Mrs Moby smiled.

'That'd be nice.'

She handed over the Allowance book as if anxious to be rid of such an incriminating document. Anne took it from her and gave her hand a squeeze. She couldn't remember squeezing Ma's hand before, though they'd often shared one paper of fish-and-chips in the old days . . . Anne saw that old room with the torn bit of carpet where Ma caught her heel . . . and sighed.

'Well – suppose I'd better be goin',' said Mrs Moby, tottering a little on her high heels. 'You won proper, didn't you?'

Anne shook her head.

'It's a treaty. I'll stay with Gran while she needs me. We'll see about anything else later. Take care, Ma. See you!'

'Chow!' said Ma, waving her hand in front of her face with would-be youthful gaiety. She walked mincingly out of the room and down the stairs.

John Lambert picked up the phone to call Miss Garfield.

Chapter 18

It was one week and one day later. Anne was alone in the house. Gran had been taken into hospital on the Friday before, ready for her operation on Monday. They had tried to say Anne must stay with the Allinsons next door, but she had not only refused, she had been so distressed that they hadn't pressed it. Anne couldn't explain how much it mattered that she should be in her own room; or how much she would mind living in a different house with old, poorly Mrs Allinson and busy Nellie. After all, she had settled in to live with Gran without any bother; and when Gran had been ill she hadn't bothered about that either, except that she had wished Gran didn't have to put up with the trouble. So how could she explain? In the end they'd compromised. Anne was to have her meals next door, but to sleep in Gran's house.

Miss Garfield and John Lambert had provided a couple of electric fires, one for her bedroom and one for the living-room, and John Lambert had come and installed them, so there was no problem of dangerous coal fires. She had stayed at Miss Garfield's house for the weekend and then they'd all called and visited Gran in hospital on the way back and taken some lovely flowers. Miss Garfield had wanted it to be roses, but roses had no scent this time of year and Gran wouldn't be able to see, she'd have to smell the flowers. In the end they had found scented carnations.

Anne stood before her dressing table, peering at the small mirror, and thinking about her visit. John Lambert and Miss Garfield seemed to be enjoying looking after her and Gran.

Then she thought about the hospital. It was an effort, because she didn't like to think about it. She had disliked it from the moment she had stepped inside the door. There was that old, familiar feeling of being trapped, as the swing door closed behind her. There were the long corridors with passages opening off and glimpses of rooms with rows of beds in them. And then Gran's room – Ward 2B they called it. Rows of high beds with little box-tables beside them, and a big table in the middle with a lot of flowers on it but all so close together you couldn't see them separately. The nurses had been nice. Young, too. But it was all too frightening. You stopped being yourself when you went in somewhere like that. You were just someone with your name.

The light was rather dim at that side of the room and Anne drew up a chair to look more closely at who she was. Here, alone in the house, she felt the need to reassure herself . . .

She could see almost no trace in the image before her of the scraggy, grubby girl with scraped-back hair who'd stolen money to go to the pictures. Her body felt different too, firm and strong and – rounded. She could remember feeling her legs were like match-sticks, in Leeds, and how big her shoes looked at the end of them.

Was she getting fat?

She moved the chair back and stood in front of the mirror, pinching her nightdress in to her figure. She liked what she saw. She wasn't skinny any more, but she was like those dancers on TV were, thin in all the right places.

What had happened to that Anne Moby? Even if she

went back to Ma, that Anne would never come back. Anne felt a moment of nostalgia for the girl she once had been.

And who was she now? Good Anne – helping them win the competition, working quite hard at school, clean and neat and tidy and looking after Gran and polite and everything. Was that Anne going to be her for ever now?

And what was going to happen to her? She turned away from the mirror and prowled round the room, trying to drive pictures from her mind by movement. She didn't want to think of Gran, high in her hospital bed, waiting for the operation tomorrow. OLD Gran, too old to have to put up with that. What would happen? Would she be all right? And even if she was, would she be able to see again? And how long would she be able to manage with only Anne to look after her, old as she was?

Anne flung herself on the bed, and almost for the first time in her life broke into a storm of tears. It was too much. The loneliness and uncertainty of her own life joined overwhelmingly with the pity of Gran's suffering and ultimate death. Because she must die one day, not so many years ahead. Everyone must die. Anne had not thought of it before, it had all seemed so many years away, unimaginably far away. But now the tragedy of what must befall them all overcame her.

Quite soon the tempest of sobs changed to quiet tears stealing down her cheeks; and then to mere sadness; and she dried her eyes, turning her pillow over to hide the wet patch, and got to her feet again, startled at the sudden collapse of her control.

She drew the chair in front of the mirror again and brushed her hair. The nights were chilly now, and the frost in the air made her hair crackle and almost spark. It shone, too. She put down the brush and looked at her face carefully.

The skin was nice and smooth. In this dim light her eyes looking back at her were mysterious and appealing.

Was she – beautiful?

Was that what she was going to be, pretty like her mother must have been, and getting married ever so young . . .?

She thought of George and William and a tingling excitement quivered over her skin.

Or would she have to use her looks to make her way if – anything happened to Gran? And her mother wouldn't keep her? She'd heard the older girls talking . . .

She wished she could go out for a walk. It was always easier to think outside, and when she was moving about. But it was late, and she was all ready for bed. If she went wandering round in the dark she might get herself into trouble and then they wouldn't let her live on her own like this . . . In fact she'd better put the light out, or they'd be saying she stayed up late and wasted the electricity . . .

She took a last look at her image in the glass, switched off the light and drew back the curtains. The window was steamy inside so she opened the casement quietly.

Suddenly she saw the whole night sky, with the full moon riding high among flying clouds. The trees of Mowbray stood dense and tall behind the church; but over them the sky was flooded with light, and the wild moon seemed to be racing . . .

What a delight!

There was all that world, all that sky.

It didn't matter if she was Ann Moby – or Anne Moby – or Anne Mowbray – or –

It didn't matter. At all. She was Anne, and this was her world.

617 296 2000 2900